finding perfect

KENDRA C. HIGHLEY

Entangled Publishing, LLC
2614 South Timberline Road
Suite 109
Fort Collins, CO 80525
Visit our website at www.entangledpublishing.com.

Crush is an imprint of Entangled Publishing, LLC.

Edited by Heather Howland
Cover design by Kelley York and Heather Howland
Cover art from Shutterstock

Manufactured in the United States of America

First Edition September 2015

For Ryan,
for always

Chapter One

Paige

"All in all," Mr. Granger said, "the scores on the midterm were pretty good, so I didn't feel the need to grade on a curve."

Paige clenched her fists in her lap, already feeling the sting of tears in the backs of her eyes. No curve? That test had read like it was written in Greek Wingdings for all she understood of it. Trying not to hyperventilate, she sneaked a few quick glances at her AP calculus classmates. Most of them didn't look worried. A few even looked relaxed and confident.

Oh God, oh God, oh God...

Mr. Granger paused by her desk. He didn't let anything show by his expression, but she could tell he was puzzled. She had a reputation of being one of the most organized, most reliable, and very best students at Alderwood. Popular, pretty, *and* smart, she'd heard people say. The girl who'd been voted Most Likely to Succeed in her class four years running.

But her teacher's expression said the exact opposite.

He slid the test onto her desk…facedown.

Facedown? She'd never had a test handed to her facedown. They didn't hand back A tests facedown. Swallowing hard, she waited until he'd moved to the desk behind hers before braving a look.

Her stomach rolled. She'd made a sixty-eight — a D. She'd gotten a *D*. She'd made exactly two Bs in her entire time at Alderwood before this semester, and so far in calc, she had two Cs and now a D on a test that was twenty-percent of her semester grade. Her final transcript was due to Stanford in January. Without at least a B in this class, she'd fall out of the top ten in her class. That might be enough for Stanford admissions to deny her application.

Calc was doing its best to ruin every dream she'd written in the little red leather notebook her mom had given her last year. Stanford for premed. Harvard for medical school. Residency with the best neurologists in Texas. Fellowship at UT Southwestern. Then go into medical practice with Daddy and take over for him when he retired. He was counting on her, and she couldn't disappoint him.

Tears welled up in her eyes while Mr. Granger went over three of the most missed questions on the exam. Ironically, she'd gotten one of those right. Even more ironic — she had no idea how. Lucky girl was lucky.

Flashes of her parents' horrified faces as they read her denial letter from Stanford kept replaying in her head. "Oh, Paige, what happened?" Mom would croon, crestfallen.

"You know your father's alma mater only takes the best."

"You tried, Sweet Pea," Daddy would say, crushing her with his inevitably sad expression. "That's what counts."

A sob threatened to tear free from her chest. How could she possibly tell them? She'd always tried to live up to their expectations and the examples they'd set—especially Daddy's. Her mother would be *so* disappointed.

Oh no, she was going to cry right here at her desk. Paige Westfield never lost her cool in public, and she wouldn't let that change now. She flung her hand in the air.

"Yes, Paige?" Mr. Granger asked.

Don't cry. Do not *cry.* "May I go to the restroom?"

Did she imagine the pity in his eyes, or was it real? "Of course."

She burst from the classroom, head down, and hurried around the corner toward the girls' bathroom at the end of senior hall. Red lockers lined the wall like witnesses to her failure. Now that she was alone, she let the tears seep down her cheeks. What was she going to do? There was no way anyone could know about this.

The hallway seemed to stretch out ahead of her, longer and longer. Would she ever make it to the safety of a bathroom stall—someplace she could silently cry her eyes out, then fix her makeup before a soul saw how upset she was? No, today was the day the universe had decided to spit in her Cheerios, because she snagged a toe on a loose spot of carpet and went sprawling. She landed flat on her stomach, arms stretched out too late to break her fall, and her breath whooshed out in one great gust.

For a moment, she couldn't do anything but force air into her lungs. Once she could breathe, though, she pushed herself to her knees, praying no one had seen her. The sound of running footsteps told her those prayers had gone spectacularly unanswered.

"Oh my God, that was a crazy fall," a guy said, sounding breathless. "You okay?"

Paige looked up at a concerned face—a boy with glasses, messy brown hair, and a frayed T-shirt. Not purposely frayed, but old and worn out, something you didn't see at Alderwood very often. "Fine," she snapped. "I'm fine."

The corner of his mouth lifted, as if he knew she couldn't stand looking foolish in front of *anyone*. "You have skid marks on your elbows and you've been crying, so I'm calling bullshit on that one."

"I was *not* crying." She glared up at him. "What are you even doing out here? Don't you have class?"

"You definitely were crying, and I could ask you the same question, Paige. My excuse is that I'm off sixth hour for work release." He held out a hand. "Here. Let me help you up."

She reached for his hand, frowning. "Do I know you?"

He rolled his eyes. "You ought to, since we've been in AP English together three of the last four years, and honors math for two."

She shook her head. "Sorry, I don't remember your name."

"No, I'd guess not, since I don't fly in your orbit." He steadied her on her feet. "My name's Ben—"

That triggered her memory. "Franklin! Ben Franklin." She laughed. "How could I forget that? Any relation, or do your parents have a sick sense of humor?"

"Both," he said, looking amused and annoyed. "So what gives? You were practically running down the hall, and you look upset. Did something happen to you?"

Her cheeks flushed hot. Was this the point when she crawled in a hole and hoped he forgot the whole thing? "No, just in a rush."

Ben cocked his head and stepped in front of her. "Are you sure that's all?"

She had to look up to see his face. God, this boy was tall, but his eyes were a warm brown behind the glasses, and he looked genuinely concerned. Some of her humiliation faded. "Yes. That's all."

He peered at her and she squirmed under the scrutiny. He seemed to see all the way down to her bones. As he put it earlier—he was totally calling bullshit on her.

"I'm fine," she repeated, wishing he would just go. She didn't know if he was the kind of guy who would happily tell his pack of science-geek friends all about this episode or not, and every minute he stared at her only made that fear worse.

"This is the part where I'm supposed to agree with you and walk away, isn't it?" he asked, that tiny smile still tugging at the corner of his mouth. "Because Paige Westfield said so, and she knows best?"

If he hadn't said that in the nicest teasing tone she'd ever heard, she might've stomped on his foot for being a jerk. "I don't know best."

"But you aren't denying that you want me to go away." He leaned against the wall of lockers. "You know, *you* could always leave. I'm fine right here."

Of all the infuriating… "I was on my way to the bathroom."

"Then go," he said. "Unless you want to talk?"

She stood there, her shoes practically glued to the rough

carpet. Her brain kept insisting that she pull it together already and walk away, but the temptation to talk to someone who might not judge her was pretty strong. "I don't know you that well."

He shrugged. "I know you. You liked *To Kill a Mockingbird* but hated *Julius Caesar* last year. You always wear a ponytail on Fridays. And you're best friends with Zoey Miller."

Okay, he was either a stalker or totally observant. "How do you know all that?"

Ben caught her eye again. "I pay attention to pretty much everything. Annoying habit, I guess."

Huh. "If I talk to you, who are you going to tell?"

"Not a soul."

Funny enough, she kind of believed him. Kind of. Even if he wasn't in her orbit, as he'd put it, Ben seemed like a nice guy. The kind of quiet, hard worker who didn't socialize much at school but never made trouble, either. The kind of boy who wouldn't make fun of her for crying or for belly-flopping in the senior hallway.

"Come on," he said with a sudden, disarming smile that made her flush again. "You can tell me what's wrong. I'm like the Fort Knox of secret keepers. Seriously."

She found herself wanting to tell him. There wasn't really anyone else to talk to. Zoey would roll her eyes and tell her not to stress, and the rest of the student council thought she was crazy for taking AP classes in general. Before she could reconsider admitting a weakness to another person, she blurted out, "I think I'm going to fail calc. None of my friends would understand—they aren't even taking math senior year. But I care *a lot*."

He nodded, and she could see her own fear of failure

lingering in his eyes. "It matters, right? Because you're on final transcript watch for college."

"Exactly." Some of the stress knotted in her shoulders relaxed. He understood—she couldn't even believe it. How did this boy she hardly knew understand her? And why hadn't she noticed him before? He was actually kind of cute—lean, with good shoulders and arms, and that sweet, quick smile. And what about the way he was looking at her? It was like he really saw *her*, not the "Perfect Paige" everyone else expected. "I don't know what I'm going to do. I left in the middle of class because I just couldn't…"

The thing was, she didn't know what to say next, but instead of letting an awkward silence grow, Ben said, "I get it. I do. I'm trying for a scholarship at A&M. I want to go to their engineering school, and I need every A I can scrape together right now."

The frayed T-shirt made a little more sense after that admission. Money wasn't her problem, but they both needed the same thing to get what they wanted. "You're not in my calculus class. Are you taking it this year?" She paused. "Of course, you have to. Engineers need it."

"Yeah, I have it third period instead of sixth."

"So you know what I mean about how hard it is."

He shifted a little, looking uncomfortable. "I…uh, I made a ninety-four on the last exam. Now, to be honest, that's my lowest grade so far, so the test was hard. But—"

He was kidding, right? *Right?* "A ninety-four? No wonder Mr. Granger said there was no curve. You blew it for the rest of us!"

He held up his hands, smiling a little. "Sorry. Math's my favorite subject. I can't help it if I'm kind of brilliant."

"'Kind of brilliant.'" She shook her head. "It takes balls to say something like that to a type-A overachiever. Because I'll make you prove it."

Ben laughed—he had a nice laugh, deep and totally real. No, there wasn't anything fake about Ben Franklin, Paige decided. What you saw was what you got, and that was different.

"You can see my grades online if you want," he said, like it was all a big joke.

"No, I believe you." She leaned against a locker and checked out the carpet burns on her elbows. God, the guys in StuCo were going to make some lovely comments about those. Good thing she was wearing jeans, because skinned knees would've been the topic of the night. "It sucks for me, though. Because now I'll never have a shot at a decent grade."

"Maybe you just need some help or something," he said, frowning. "You're not stupid, Paige. And math is solvable."

"Did you just make a math joke about math?" she asked. Of course he did. "I tried going in for tutoring with Mr. Granger. If anything, he confused me more. Maybe he's just a sucky teacher."

"No," Ben said in a voice that suggested she was acting like a five-year-old. "He's a good teacher. Calculus is just one of those subjects that can be hard to understand at first. It's only October. It's been what, nine weeks?"

"Yes, and nine weeks from now we have semester exams!" Her pulse stuttered and her lungs felt tight. Maybe she should find a paper bag to breathe into. "I'm doomed."

"That's a little melodramatic, don't you think? What about asking a friend from class to help you? Maybe someone could explain it better than Mr. Granger. Sometimes it's easier to learn from a peer than from your teacher."

She gave him a questioning look. "What, you mean… *you*?"

"What? Uh, no." Ben's eyebrows shot nearly to his hairline. "I meant for you to ask one of the…uh, the…"

"It's okay, you can say 'popular kids' without it sounding like a slam." Sure, she was popular by default because of her best friend, but that didn't mean she felt like she was one of them. "First off, none of them are taking calc. And second, they can't know I'm having trouble. No one can. There are plenty of people who would love to hear all about my failures in math."

"If your friends think you failing a class is funny, they suck," he muttered.

"Maybe, but I can't even tell my parents. My father… well, he's the one who wants me to go to Stanford, and if I'm failing, he'll be so disappointed. I *can't* disappoint him. And my mom…she doesn't understand failure. Like, not at all." She took a shuddering breath, scared she might cry again. "I can't screw this up, Ben."

His expression faded into something sympathetic. "I know a little about that kind of thing."

Did his mom and dad have high standards, too? "I bet you do."

"Yeah…" He paused, looking deep in thought. It was funny—he looked almost nervous, plucking at the frayed hem of his T-shirt. "Okay, I'll do it."

"Do what?" she asked.

"Tutor you," he said.

She sucked in a breath. Oh, she hadn't meant… "That's

nice, but…uh…"

"I'm the best tutor you're going to find, Paige," Ben said. "You can trust me on that one."

Would this work? Could it work? She didn't know, but it was worth asking what he'd charge while she thought about it—and looked for other options, just in case.

"I can pay you," she said. He could probably use the money, right? "Most of my tutors charge twenty bucks an hour. How's that?"

"I work two jobs. I can always use more money, but I can work more hours, too." Ben was watching her, his forehead wrinkled in concentration. "I was thinking about a knowledge trade instead."

What kind of knowledge did she have that he didn't? "Like what?"

He bit his lip. "It's kind of weird."

This might end in pain, but desperate girls took desperate action. "Okay…let's hear it."

Chapter Two

Ben

Paige stared at him, a skeptical look on her face. And why not—Ben, some crazy math geek, had appeared out of nowhere to witness her falling down in the hallway. Her angst over being caught in an embarrassing moment made him feel bad—she really didn't like anyone seeing her being less than perfect. He'd always admired her spirit—she was one of the few rich kids around here who wanted to succeed as much as he did. And she worked hard for it. He respected that. And now—now he could be her knight in shining armor. Armed with a graphing calculator and a sharp pencil, he would help her pass calc...and maybe get something even better in return.

Who knew forgetting his physics book would've been the best thing to happen to him all senior year? He was going to be late for work at the tire store, and there would be hell to pay with Kent, but this was too perfect a chance to miss. Paige was in trouble, and he could help her out of it. The hard part would be convincing her to help him with a quest he'd had since his sophomore year—going on a date with Zoey Miller, the blond goddess of all his daydreams.

The problem was, Zoey was upper-stratosphere popular. Like homecoming queen, student council president, every-one-was-in-love-with-her popular. Like if there was a su-preme deity of Alderwood High, she'd be sitting at its right hand, passing out blessings to the mere mortals around her. It took a crazy-special guy to be in her league.

And he…wasn't. He wasn't bottom caste, because he kept his head down at school, but he definitely wasn't her type. No, she probably liked guys who looked—and dressed—like Hollister models. Guys who played football and drove new cars. Ben wouldn't even be a blip on her radar.

Until now.

He had no idea if Paige was going to agree, but he knew that even if she said no, she wouldn't tell anyone about this. She'd told him a secret, right? It was only fair that he tell her one. There shouldn't be too many consequences for asking for a really insane favor. "You're Zoey Miller's best friend—"

Paige's eager expression faded into suspicion. "God, not you, too. If I had a quarter for every guy who asked me about Zoey, I wouldn't need Stanford. Seriously, why her?"

Ben's heart thumped painfully in his chest. Why Zoey? Because he'd stared at her from across the cafeteria, won-dering what it would be like to sit next to her. Because pass-ing her in the hallway made his pulse leap like nothing else did. Because he wasn't part of her world, and it would take a miracle for her to notice him.

And he was fresh out of miracles.

But now…now his miracle was standing right in front of him, and flunking calculus. Paige Westfield, the catapult for the best date of his life.

He took a breath, trying to steady himself. The last thing he needed was to look like some freak…or a stalker. "In exchange for tutoring you, I was hoping you could set me up with her."

"Set you up? Like, to hang out?"

"Yes. Just me and her."

"Like…a date?" she asked.

"Um, yeah."

She was staring at him like he'd turned into a flying monkey. "I don't understand. Why would you want a date with Zoey in exchange for tutoring me?"

"That's my business." He ran a hand through his hair, sure he was starting to sound like a grade-A creeper. "Look, I'm good enough at calculus to help you pull your grade up to at least a B before the end of the semester. All I want in exchange is one date with Zoey. Not the chance to ask her out—an actual date."

Now Paige was scowling. "That's…that's…"

"A bargain," Ben said, hoping he didn't sound like he was begging. He hated charity in all forms—part of the reason he was working two jobs to save money for college—but if this was a business proposition, then that was different. "One date."

"How do you expect me to do that?" she asked, sounding indignant. "Do you have any idea what Zoey is like? She doesn't date high school guys. Like, almost never. She's very particular about what she wants in a guy, and no one here has made the cut since sophomore year."

Which was why this was his only chance. Zoey was somewhat of a mystery—rumor was that she only dated college guys, and she went to dances with friends, so no one knew for sure. But he'd had a crush on her for two long years, and time was running out.

"That's why I need your help." He picked at the frayed spot on his T-shirt again. "I need you to do two things: one, make me into someone Zoey might go out with. Two, help me get to know her so I can ask her out without it being random."

"No way." Paige started walking back toward the calculus classroom. "That's like asking me to be Zoey's pimp or something."

"It's not," Ben said, falling into step next to her. "You're playing matchmaker. You can dress me up, teach me how to act around Zoey, and make sure she notices me. That's all you have to do. I'll take care of the rest."

She stopped and put a hand on her hip. Ben had to admit her fierceness was kind of cute. She was tiny, only coming up to his collarbone, and her dark brown hair seemed to have a life of its own, curling around her shoulders like it was as mad at him as she was. She resembled an angry fairy, and he couldn't hold back a smile at the thought of her with a pair of gossamer wings, carrying a nightstick instead of a wand, to smack people on the head for unacceptable behavior.

Now she narrowed her eyes like she knew what he was thinking. "Are you sure cash isn't acceptable?"

His hope shriveled up into a tiny ball and retreated to the corner of his brain to wait this out, rather than be dashed on the floor. How could he possibly expect her to understand what it was like, since they all lived on the country club side of Alderwood, far away from the auto shops, farm equipment stores, and 7-Elevens on his side of town? How would "Perfect Paige" know what it was like to work two jobs and still not have money for anything? To be invisible to anyone and everyone because he wore secondhand jeans and T-shirts his mother bought at Walmart. She couldn't, and that was the problem.

"No," he said, ready to say to hell with the whole thing. Her father could bribe her way into Stanford. "I don't want money. I want to stop being like wallpaper around here."

"What's this really about? You want to be popular or something? Because, trust me, you don't."

"How would you have any idea?" he shot back. "I'm not asking you to arrange for me to have sex with Zoey. I just want to become someone she'd notice, that's all."

Whatever he expected for an answer, he sure didn't expect to see a resigned, tired look in Paige's eyes. "Becoming one of those guys isn't all you think it is."

"Not what?" Ben asked. "Popular? Rich? Liked by everyone? Because I can tell you from my side of things that it's worth it."

She stared at her hands like she didn't want to agree with him. "You know what, never mind. Does it really mean that much to you?"

"Yes." His heart shot into his throat and his hope crept out of storage to see what might happen. "It means that much to me."

Paige sighed, and it sounded incredibly sad, but she said, "Okay. I'll think about it. This isn't a promise, though."

"Perfect!" He could see the wheels turning in Paige's head. She was really considering the deal, and he needed to close it before she changed her mind. He dug a piece of paper out of his pocket, along with a stubby pencil, and scrawled his number on it. "You can text or call whenever you decide."

She took the paper in two fingers, like she was already regretting this conversation, but she slipped it into the pocket of her jeans. "I will. Now, I'd better go back to class before Mr. Granger thinks I died in the bathroom." She paused. "You're sure about this?"

"Yeah," Ben answered. "I'm sure."

Paige started down the hallway. "We'll just see about that."

Chapter Three

PAIGE

Paige walked back to calculus in a daze, taking it slow in case the scratchy indoor/outdoor carpet in the hall decided to enact more revenge on her. She'd finally met a guy who seemed real, who made her feel—just for a second—that it was okay not to be totally put together every second of every day.

Then he asked about Zoey.

Of *course* he asked about Zoey.

Every damn guy in the universe asked about Zoey.

She couldn't remember not being her best friend's wing-man. Or was it wing-person? Oh, who cared? It didn't matter where they were: the mall, the beach in Corpus Christi, or a kegger at Jace Tillman's house. Zoey—blond-haired, blue-eyed, perfect body—stopped traffic. Paige had always been content with that. She was the cute, reliable, smart one, while

Zoey was the gorgeous, daring, fun one. But something about Ben liking Zoey, well, that hurt. Ben seemed like the kind of guy who should like *her*, not Zoey.

She should've said no flat out, rather than promising to think about it. She wasn't in the Get Zoey a Date business. Besides, getting her to talk to Ben would be a nightmare. Zoey had some strict rules about the guys she associated with—and that was merely to be friends with her. She did *not* date Alderwood boys. Would Ben be satisfied with a friends-only date? Or could Paige convince Zoey to break from tradition and go out with him?

Somehow, neither of those things seemed likely.

Paige could fix Ben's hair, at least. He just needed a decent haircut. But what about the rest? Could she even do this? Could she do what he asked, even if she thought it wouldn't make him happy? Even if she thought it would be a giant pain in the ass?

She took a deep breath and went back into calculus. Mr. Granger was talking about absolute convergence. Having missed part of his lecture, to her, his problem on the whiteboard made no sense. None. She slipped into her metal desk. It wasn't like it would've made sense if she'd been here the whole time, either.

Paige bit her lip hard enough to sting. She had no choice…if she wanted to pass this Godforsaken excuse for a math class, she needed Ben Franklin. And to get Ben Franklin, she had to remake him into the kind of guy Zoey would hook up with.

Damn it.

It didn't matter that he was cute. Passing calc was more important. Stanford was more important. If becoming a clone of popular guys like Jace was what Ben wanted, then that's what she'd do. And she'd try to convince her best friend to give him a second look. Even if she didn't like the idea.

She'd text him tonight. No sense in seeming too eager— let him sweat a little. Maybe he'd decide he wanted the money more.

Luckily the bell rang ten minutes later. She was the first person out of class, huddling around the stack of books in her arms as she navigated the hallway. Her afternoon and evening were jammed solid, and she needed to leave so she could practice her sonata for the senior piano recital before the StuCo meeting. If she did that, then she might be able to tackle her mountain of homework afterward and still have time to sleep. Assuming Jace didn't keep the council tied up with stupid stories about the football team. He'd better not—she was on a schedule.

"Hey, you okay?"

Zoey materialized next to Paige's locker. Her own locker was two doors down, which made Paige escaping unseen nearly impossible. "Yeah, fine."

Zoey frowned. "Then why do you look like someone stole a basket full of kittens out of your locker to hold them for ransom?"

"Basket full of kittens…ha." Paige dove into her locker to avoid looking at her. "We're still on for the meeting tonight?"

"Yep, six sharp. Don't be late."

That drew a real laugh, and Paige looked around her locker door, smiling. "When have I ever been late?"

Zoey's left eyebrow went up. If Paige did that, she'd

look like a French mime. Zoey? She looked mysteriously skeptical. "Never. Are you sure you're all right?"

"Fine!" Paige knew her voice sounded more fake than their friend Jessica's breasts—and the girl had "expanded" two cup sizes over the summer—but she had too much to process and needed to escape before she blurted out, "Ben Franklin thinks you're hot." She forced a cheery smile. "In fact, I was just thinking about bringing cookies to the meeting. Mom still has us on that ridiculous diet, and I need sugar."

"Chocolate chip?"

"What else?"

The eyebrow was still in play, but Zoey let her off with an, "Okay. See you later."

Paige nodded, then made a break for the parking lot. The hallway was choked with people trying to leave for the day, and it should've been easy to disappear into the crush.

"Paige!" Alana Peterson was pushing through the crowd, waving at her. She was wearing a bright orange and pink Lilly Pulitzer dress, which made it hard for Paige to pretend she hadn't seen her. She stood out like a Caribbean beach resort in the gray-carpeted, white-walled main hallway.

So much for disappearing. "Hey."

Alana's sandals thumped, muffled against the carpet, as she hurried over. "I'm so glad I caught you. The honor society wants to plan a fall social, and we'd love your help organizing it."

Help. Right. That was code for "Ask Paige and she'll do it all." She held in a sigh. At least this kind of thing looked good on her college applications. "I'd be happy to help. When are we meeting?"

"Week after next," Alana said.

"Text me the details and I'll put it on the calendar." Without waiting for a response, she turned and bolted for the door. By the time she made it out to her Mustang, a gift from Daddy for making a 2100 on her SATs, her stomach was aching again. Dozens of students milled around the parking lot, laughing and calling to one another, not a care in the world. Alderwood High—a brick square of a public school masquerading as a private school, full of students with enough money not to have to care about the things they weren't interested in. Which was why she often felt like a black cat in a room full of Pomeranians.

Why had Ben asked for such a crazy favor? How could she possibly make him over *and* get Zoey to notice him? He wasn't her type.

He's my *type*.

That was the hellacious thing about all this. He was the type of guy she'd always hoped to meet in college. Cute, but not so cute that he was cocky about it. Sweet, but not a pushover. She needed a strong personality to keep her on her toes. And smart, so she had someone interesting to talk to.

From the little bit she'd seen of Ben, he seemed to be most, and possibly all, of those things.

Maybe it was just as well that he liked Zoey. Paige didn't need romantic entanglements right now. She had a transcript to rock, an admission to earn, and a future to create. Since being accepted into Stanford was the important thing, she'd go along with Ben's request and hope she made an A in calculus for her trouble.

A wave of exhaustion nearly bowled her over, and Paige

rested her head on the steering wheel. Why did everything seem so hopeless despite all her careful plans? And what the hell was she still doing here, sitting in the parking lot?

Cursing under her breath, she drove home, expecting her life to start going the way she'd planned by the time she hit her driveway.

Chapter Four

Ben raced to his locker after Paige walked off. That had to have been the weirdest conversation ever, but if she could find a way to help him ask Zoey out, he'd be able to leave Alderwood High without any regrets. He'd spent so much time working and ignoring everything around him, it felt like he'd missed half of high school. One date with Zoey…now that would give him something great to remember, instead of just some cheesy academic awards. It might also make people remember *him*: the only guy to go out with the Goddess Herself senior year.

Wouldn't that show everyone he wasn't a shadow on the wall?

Besides, teaching a smart girl how to do calculus would be *easy*. He didn't know what Paige's mental block was, but it had to be just that. If she'd only relax, he bet she'd do fine.

Which meant he had the better end of this deal.

He shoved his physics book into his backpack and headed to the bike rack with only thirty minutes left to make it to the tire store. He'd have to push hard to make the five-mile ride across town.

Ben unchained his bike and navigated out of the parking lot, dodging cars and trucks until he made it onto the trails that cut across the greenbelt, dividing the rich side of Alderwood from the other side. The working-class side. *His* side. Paige probably had a swimming pool in her backyard and a country-club membership, while he lived in a two-bedroom house built in 1961, made out of cinderblock and withered dreams.

Not forever, a little voice insisted in his head. *Not too much longer.*

Ben pedaled harder, not caring as sweat beaded on his forehead and ran down his back. It was hot for early October, but North Texas didn't really have fall. Besides, it wasn't like his job required him to be squeaky-clean. No, the customers at Smith Tire and Auto expected him to look like a grease monkey, so the sweat was practically an accessory.

The woods flew by in a sea of green, leaves rustling in the wake left by his bike. The creek murmured cheerfully as he passed. A jolt of surprise hit him every time he noticed the water in it. They'd just broken a long drought, but for the first three years he was at Alderwood, the creek had been a thin trickle surrounded by cracked earth. Maybe it was a sign of better things to come.

The physics book in his backpack was grinding a hole in his hip, but he didn't feel like stopping long enough to fix it. If he wanted to ride in the Hotter'n Hell Hundred marathon next summer, the corner of a physics book couldn't be enough to slow him down.

He made it to the garage with five minutes to spare and swung a leg over his bike to glide to a stop while balanced on one pedal. Kent had put in a bike rack next to the service entrance just for him early in the summer. "Define irony," Kent had said. "A bike rack at a tire store."

"Bikes have tires," Ben had protested.

"So do strollers, but we sell serious radials here, kid."

Ben smiled, remembering that conversation as he shoved his way through the employees-only door at the back of the shop. The locker area/break room always smelled like motor oil and engine exhaust despite the pine-tree-shaped air freshener hanging from the air conditioning vent. He dumped his backpack in his cubby and pulled on his coveralls. BEN was printed on a patch on the front.

He stared at it for a moment, unable to control the frustration sparking through his veins. He couldn't get around the fact: he was a mechanic.

"Not forever," he whispered, looking longingly at his backpack. So what if it took working two jobs the rest of senior year? He was going to Texas A&M to study engineering if it killed him.

"Yo, Franklin," Juan, the garage supervisor, called. "You coming to work today or not, man?"

"Yeah, I'm coming." He grabbed his safety glasses and followed Juan out into the garage bay. An SUV was already up on the rack, and four more cars were waiting their turns. "What, did everyone decide to run over nails today?"

Juan laughed. "Seems like it."

It took thirty minutes to fix the SUV with four new

tires. By the time they lowered it and Juan drove it to the customer lot, Kent came out to check on them. "Ben, I need you up front. We're slammed and I need someone to write up orders."

Ben looked down at his smudged coveralls. He hated working the customer desk. People were always in a hurry, rude, and looked at him funny. "Do I have to?"

Kent threw up his hands. "No, of course not. But I don't have to pay you, either."

"All right, all right."

Ben followed his boss inside and took his place at the desk. Once he found an order form and a pen, he called out, "Next!" without looking up.

"Hi," a soft, breathy voice said. "I have a flat."

His head popped up. Oh God—it was Zoey Miller. Like a python, her blue eyes could mesmerize mere mortals, and he was definitely not immune. Today she had on a white mini-skirt and a tight pink polo he couldn't help staring at. A flush spread across his cheeks as he realized she was seeing him in his sweaty, grease-stained coveralls. Maybe she wouldn't notice him or remember they went to school together…

She giggled softly. "Think I could buy a new tire?"

"What? Oh, um, yes. Anything special? We have a great selection."

We have a great selection? This was the first time she'd addressed him directly, other than asking him to sign some bogus petition junior year, and that's all he could think of saying? What the hell?

She looked confused. "No…I just need one that matches the other three. My dad said you should carry them." Zoey pointed toward the parking lot. "I can show you what I mean, if you want."

Yes, he did want. He'd follow her anywhere and enjoy the view. "Lead the way."

She gave him another funny glance, shook her head, and led him out to a pretty white BMW 3 Series with a spare tire on the front left. Ben knelt down to check the regular tire's specs, and she asked, "So you have them?"

"Yes," he said. "Come back inside and we'll write it up."

As they walked back, Ben's brain was shouting, *Say something! Do something! Anything!*

But his tongue remained paralyzed. Yep, he looked like a complete idiot, staring at a pretty girl without saying a word. He hurried behind the sales desk and filled out the tire information. "Could you fill out the top portion?"

She grabbed his pen, brushing her fingers against his hand. "So...when will it be ready?"

Ben's pulse lurched at her touch. He checked the clock. "Um, we close in three hours and we're really backed up, so it might be tomorrow."

Damn if tears didn't spring up in her eyes. "This can't be happening. I have a student council meeting in ninety minutes. Is there anything you can do?"

Here was his chance to impress her, but if Kent found out, he'd be toast. Still, it was *Zoey Miller*. "I'll see if I can work you in. Just have a seat, and I'll let you know."

Her smile nearly knocked him over. "My hero."

He smiled back, feeling like his brain had fried. "I'll be right back."

As soon as she went to the waiting room, Ben dodged through the sales team and ran out into the garage bay. "Juan! Juan!"

Juan slid out from underneath a minivan. He had a stripe of motor oil across one plump cheek. "What? Uh-oh, what's with the begging face?"

"There's a girl here; she's the hottest girl in school, and she needs her car pronto. Think we could work her in off cycle?" Ben asked, his words tumbling out in a rush. "I'm not too proud to beg on this one."

Juan's expression was kind, but he shook his head. "You're talking about the blonde, right?" Seeing Ben's startled look, he smiled. "We all saw her come in. I know you want to help her, but we're way behind, and her crocodile tears aren't gonna get anywhere with me."

"But—"

Juan patted Ben's shoulder. "You know I love you, man, but you need to face it—she's out of your league, and she's just using you to get what she wants. It's not worth pissing off Kent. Once you're a little older, you'll see it yourself."

Frustration welled up in Ben's chest, but he knew Juan was right—and that sucked.

Praying that Paige could work miracles where all he could do was fail, Ben went out to the waiting room to tell Zoey her car would be ready tomorrow.

Chapter Five

Paige arrived in the meeting room at the Alderwood town library fifteen minutes early. As secretary of the student council, her job was to make sure everyone had last month's minutes and the agenda. It was a responsible job, so of course she'd been elected to serve.

No one had bothered to run against her.

After leaving a copy of all the paperwork at each place — each set out in a perfectly straight pile, and parallel to the edge of the table — Paige sank down in her chair. The cookies she'd brought smelled like little bits of chocolate heaven, but her stomach was roiling too much to convince her to try one. She ran sweaty hands over her jeans. Hopefully the meeting wouldn't take too long. She had to finish her homework. And nine hundred other things.

Thinking about it brought the stupid calculus test to

the front of her mind. It had been so hard. Math had always been her "trouble" subject, but with extra studying, she'd scraped A's in geometry, algebra II, and pre-calc. It had been a struggle, though, and now she was afraid she'd hit the wall on her abilities. What would Mom say if she came home with a B or, God forbid, a C?

She could just imagine the look on her face, because lately, Mom was harder and harder to impress. The last day she could remember her mother being truly proud of her was when she announced she'd go to medical school. She'd been a freshman then, taking honors biology (and acing it, thank you very much). Daddy had been ecstatic. Within five minutes, he'd had her whole future mapped out. College. Medical school. Residency. And finally, taking over his practice. It all sounded perfect, especially to him and Mom. Which made all of this harder.

Paige sighed. It wasn't that she didn't want to be a doctor—she did—but why was it so important she go to Stanford instead of the University of Texas or Baylor? Both of those schools had excellent premed and medical programs, and they were much closer to home. She was a Texan, and California was so far away.

But Daddy went to Stanford, which meant she was going to Stanford. End of story.

Unless she didn't get in.

"Whew, I made it," Zoey said, blowing into the room like a strong summer wind to interrupt Paige's wallow in self-pity. "I thought I was going to be late. I couldn't get my car fixed today, which totally sucked. I even tried playing damsel in distress with the guy at the counter, but that didn't work. Mom had to pick me up like I was a twelve-year-old stuck at the skating rink."

"That's too bad," Paige mumbled.

"You're not even going to scold me for trying to work the system at the tire place?" Zoey said, looking concerned. "And this is the second time in"—she checked her phone—"three hours that I've seen you nearly in tears. What's going on?"

"Nothing." She smiled, praying her lips wouldn't tremble and give her away. "I'm just thinking about all the homework I have."

Zoey rested her chin on her fist. "God. That would make anyone cry. You're a senior. You're supposed to pad your course load with easy classes. Why did you torture yourself with a full schedule?"

"This semester is my last chance at Stanford. After this semester I can dial it back a little."

"I hope so, because you're the only seventeen-year-old I know who looks like she's about to stroke out from stress." Zoey picked up a cookie and took a huge bite, smearing a little bit of chocolate in the corner of her mouth. "Yum. Almost as good as sex," she said with a grin.

The door banged open and Jace Tillman came strutting into the room, flipping his sandy hair like a boy-band reject. "Almost? I'll take that as a compliment."

Paige rolled her eyes. Jace was one of those guys who belonged on the heartthrob page of *Seventeen* magazine for middle schoolers to pin on their bedroom walls. Broad shoulders, carved arms, and white teeth, all in one cocky, condescending package.

Zoey scoffed with a dubious eyebrow raise. "You shouldn't. And I would know."

"Hey, I've been told I've upped my game since sopho-more year." He leaned close to her and wiped the chocolate from her mouth. "Want to find out if it's true?"

Paige ground her teeth. Oh, he wasn't. He was *not* playing Zoey, was he? He'd broken her heart into tiny pieces and stomped all over them with his cleats two years ago. That's when she stopped dating Alderwood boys.

Paige had to stop this before it got out of hand. "How's Kaitlyn?"

Jace gave her a sharp glance. "Um, she's fine. I guess."

"You *guess*?" she said. "How can you not know how your girlfriend is?"

His expression closed off, hinting at the darkness lurking in that pretty body. "Because we broke up, *Perfect Paige*. So I'm a free agent, and it's none of your goddamned business."

Her mouth dropped open at his harsh tone. Before she could say anything about him snapping at her, Zoey jumped in, her face cold. "Leave her alone. She didn't know you two broke up."

Jace held up his hands and let a sad smile unfreeze his features. "Hey, sorry. I'm still reeling, you know?"

Oh, for God's sake. He was going for the sympathetic, I-need-comfort play. Surely Zoey would see right through that.

Instead, her mouth turned down in an empathetic frown. She walked over and put a hand on his arm. "I'm sorry. You two were good together."

Paige stifled a groan. She loved Zoey, but she really wished she'd widen her horizons where guys were con-cerned. Making Ben into her Dream Date Ken doll would be a tall, tall order. But he was better than the alternative, assuming Zoey was falling for Jace's crap and not just toying with him.

Maybe this whole project would be a good thing after all.

Luckily, she was saved from watching Jace attempt more flirting by the entrance of the rest of the council. As soon as they sat down, everyone started arguing about the homecoming dance. Paige's head began to pound. They were never going to make it out of here in time for her to finish everything before midnight. Holding in a sigh, she opened her laptop and prepared to take minutes.

Chapter Six

Ben

Zoey's face when Ben had told her there was nothing he could do about her tire... Damn. She'd looked at him like the grease monkey he was. Then, pouting, she'd called her mom to pick her up. Any thought he might've had about coming to her rescue was gone. No chance of her remembering his name or noticing that he was a senior at Alderwood just like her. No hope she might hear him say something funny, laugh, and decide he was worth knowing.

And that was the problem, wasn't it, he thought while removing the lug nuts from a flat on an F-150 that looked like it had taken every muddy back road into town. He glanced down at his coveralls—this was how she saw him. Covered in mud and grease, invisible in his mechanic's clothes, and hidden behind glasses and an eight-dollar haircut. His mom kept telling him he had such potential. That one day he'd be remembered by history as a famous inventor, just like "Great-Uncle Ben."

Maybe he *would* be a famous inventor someday—he worked hard enough. For now, though, it would be nice to have a girl look at him the way they looked at Jace Tillman. The guy's brain was a freaking rock, but girls almost fainted when he walked the halls.

He chuckled darkly. His dad had been a Jace Tillman back in the day. Mom had thrown away most of his pictures when he walked out on them, but Ben remembered enough to know he was a good-looking guy. From a rich family, too, where he'd been the black sheep…which was why Ben and his mom were dead broke. Did his grandparents even know his name or care about him at all? Maybe that's why he was so driven to succeed—to prove to the Franklins that he was worth being part of the family. That could also be why going out with Zoey was so important to him. It would prove he'd made it.

And now he was psychoanalyzing himself at work. Daddy issues? Check. Low self-esteem? Check. Idiot around gorgeous girls? Check, check, effing check.

God, taking psychology second period was a mistake.

It was after seven when he finished up at work, and fully dark by the time he turned his bike onto his street. Half the streetlights were out, so he navigated by porch lights, counting the ones he knew worked until he came to the little two-bedroom house he shared with his mom.

After he locked his bike in the carport, he went into the dark house. The car was gone, but that wasn't a surprise. Mom was working the dinner shift at the club tonight. She'd left him some spaghetti, he noticed when he went into the kitchen to forage for dinner, along with a Post-It stuck to the Formica countertop, with a little heart on it. They might not have much, but she made sure he had a home-cooked dinner as often as she could.

He took a quick shower, then heated up dinner in their microwave and settled down at the dinette table between the tiny kitchen and living room. Their "dining area" was the strip of carpet dividing the kitchen from the sofa, but the overhead light was bright, and the tabletop was big enough to spread out his books. For a while, he let the creak of his old chair, the faint hum of the fluorescent bulbs, and the scratch of his pencil erase the hopelessness from earlier. Homework, he understood.

So, naturally, he was annoyed when his phone buzzed, breaking his flow. He picked it up and glanced at the screen, thinking it might be Adam or Evan looking for help in physics. It was an unfamiliar number, though, and when he read the message, his heart started to race.

It's Paige. I'm in. You free tomorrow?

Yes! Grinning, he texted back: *After six.*

Meet me at the library.

He pumped a fist in the air. She was going to do it. Maybe the now-full creek was right—better things were on the way. Humming happily, he went back to studying.

A few hours later, he looked up and stretched. Eleven twenty. Mom would be home soon, and she'd nag if he wasn't in bed. He rushed through brushing his teeth and stripping down to boxers and a T-shirt. Before going to bed, he gave himself a once-over in the mirror. His arms were bulking up after hauling tires onto cars all day long, and his shoulders were, too. Plus, all that time outside on his bike and working, with limited lunch breaks, had leaned out his abs and tanned his skin. So what if he didn't play football—he had the body for it. The problem was everything else: the cheap frames of his glasses, the constant cowlick in his hair, the grease under his nails. Maybe Fairy Godmother Paige would figure out how to fix some of that on a limited—*very* limited—budget.

Ben snorted and turned off the bathroom light. He should just give up and take the cash for tutoring Paige. She had the money, and that route was less likely to end in humiliation. At least on his part. Still, the thought of walking into one of *their* parties with Zoey and having people notice he was there…that would be something, wouldn't it?

The front door banged closed. A few seconds later, his mother called, "Benji? Why are you still up?"

He dove into bed, grabbing a book just before Mom poked her head in. "Reading."

She smiled. "Good boy, always reading. But you need your rest."

He could argue the same about her. She'd been working doubles lately, and it showed. Her thin shoulders were bowed, and her wispy brown hair was a chaotic wreck. "Rough shift?"

She just smiled like she always did. She'd already taken off her shoes, even though she still wore her uniform—a tailored pair of black pants and a button-down red shirt. "Busy. You'd think a Tuesday night would be slow, but everyone seemed to want to have dinner at the club tonight."

Her voice was bright and cheery—never a good sign.

"What happened?"

"It's nothing," she said, sounding wearier. "Your usual group of jackass businessmen out on the town. One of them grabbed Maggie's behind, made her cry. So I 'accidentally' spilled his iced tea in his lap."

Ben sat up. A grin spread across his face. "You didn't!"

"I did." She sighed, and it ended with a chuckle. "I also got written up and pulled off weekends for the next month. Paul knew the guy deserved it, so they aren't firing me, at least."

Concern raced through him, making his limbs tingle. "But…no weekends. Are we going to make rent? Your tips will be down."

"Don't you worry about that." Mom went to close his bedroom door. "Get some sleep. I expect you rested so you can keep those grades high."

He nodded, numb, but after she left, a pit opened in his stomach. He could help out—he had savings—but if he did, would he have enough to enroll at A&M next year? Even with financial aid and scholarships, it was going to be tight, but covering the rent and helping Mom out was more important. He could always work his way through school.

Why couldn't something go easily for a change?

No, worrying about it wouldn't fix anything. Tomorrow he'd talk to Kent and see about working a few hours Saturday mornings before his shift at the movie theater.

And he'd tell Paige he'd rather have the cash. Figuring out how to make Zoey notice him would have to wait.

Chapter Seven

PAIGE

"Paige, is that you?" Mom called as soon as Paige walked through the front door.

"Yes." Paige rubbed her eyes, then hung her keys on the hook next to the coat stand in the entryway. She wanted nothing more than to climb the stairs right in front of her, put on her PJs, and sleep. It was already past eleven, but sleep wasn't on the list until she drafted an essay for English, emailed the ElderCare center about the bake sale she'd organized to raise money for a new rec room piano, and studied for an exam in Spanish IV.

"Honey?" Mom had come into the entryway from the living room around the corner. Worry lines creased her forehead. "Are you all right?"

Why did everyone keep asking her that? Then again, she was staring into space at the foot of the stairs. "Yes, sorry. I was just thinking." She smiled at her mom. What had started out as a reassuring, fake smile turned into a grin. "Did you know you have flour on your cheek?"

Her mom was dressed in yoga pants, a Life Gym T-shirt, and running shoes. Her ash-blond hair was coming out of the ponytail at the base of her neck and, yes, there was a streak of flour on her face…and on her pants, in the shape of a handprint.

Paige started giggling. "*What* have you been doing?"

"Making low-fat brownies for your bake sale." Mom dusted the flour off her cheek. "Tomorrow I'm going to bake some gluten-free cookies. Not everyone will want those sugar-filled treats."

Leave it to her mother to bake health-conscious desserts for a fund-raiser. Between Daddy's near-religious stance on moderation being the key to good health and Mom's status as Pinterest's Queen of Healthy Eating, Paige had to buy her candy bars in the vending machine at school.

"Thanks," she told her. "Every little bit helps."

"It certainly does. The center will really appreciate that piano. I've read that having instruments handy can help Alzheimer's patients."

Paige nodded. "Even if they can't remember who they are, sometimes they can still play, and it's soothing." She put a foot on the stairs, hoping Mom would take the hint. "I need to go email them and make sure everything is good to go, then do some homework."

"Okay. Make sure you rest, though. You've looked tired lately." Mom turned back toward the kitchen. "I'll whip up a cucumber facial cream to refresh your complexion."

Paige held in a groan. Mom was forever coming up with

some new-age, organic, natural remedy to fix something a few hours of good sleep could cure. "Maybe on the weekend. I have to be at school early tomorrow."

"All right, but don't forget to pick up your dress for the recital. The tailor said the alterations are almost done." She frowned. "You have been practicing, right? I haven't heard you playing very much lately, and the recital's a week from today. Maybe you should make time tonight?"

Really? It was almost midnight. "I've been practicing at school. And I promise to pick up the dress." With that, she made her escape. She nearly had the recital piece down cold anyway. It was Beethoven's "Sonata Op. 49 in G Minor," and while the allegro still tripped her up in a few spots, it was almost right.

She flopped on her bed, eager to dump the whole I've-got-it-all-together routine and just be quiet and messy for a while. No one understood how much effort it took to be effortless. She knew the others called her "Perfect Paige" just like Jace. Zoey probably did, too, behind her back. For a long time, she'd seen it as a compliment—they had their drama while she had her destiny.

Now, she wasn't so sure. What good was the act if she was so, so tired underneath?

She had to find a way to pass calculus or everything she'd worked for would evaporate, leaving nothing but *Imperfect* Paige behind. What would Ben think about the real her? The girl who bought M&M's at the convenience store and hid them in her purse so her mother wouldn't catch her with junk food? Or the girl who would rather play covers of Imagine Dragons on her piano than Beethoven...but still loved Beethoven, too? Would he laugh at her? Or would he understand that she was weird inside?

Her friends wouldn't. She had to play their game, and now, she had to play it perfectly to help Ben get what he wanted, even if it bothered her.

The front door banged closed downstairs. "I'm home!"

Paige sat up fast and paused just long enough to make sure her cheeks weren't blotchy before hurrying to the banister to wave hello to Daddy. Even from upstairs, you could tell he was a big man—six-three and two hundred pounds of muscle—and handsome, too, with the same dark hair as Paige and rich brown eyes. Even though it was late, he still wore his dress pants and button-down shirt, with his starched white lab coat slung over his arm.

"How was your day?" she called.

"Pretty cool, actually," he said, smiling up at her. "Mr. Kennedy came by."

Her mood improved. "Oh, I love him! How is he?"

"The experimental treatments have done some good. His motor control is improving, and he recognizes his son again. This is it, Sweet Pea. This is why we do what we do, okay? These are the days that make all the studying and hard work and late nights worth it."

Her dad's stories were why she'd decided on a career in medicine. That, and seeing the patients improve. "I'm so glad," she said. "I'll go see him before the bake sale tomorrow afternoon."

"Good. The residents always enjoy your visits."

He went through to the living room, calling for Mom, and Paige went back to her room. *These are the days*, he'd said. Maybe she wasn't entirely sure she would make it through college and medical school, but she would try.

No pressure, right? Only the responsibility of other people's lives in her hands.

She shivered. Yeah, that kind of put things into perspective, didn't it? She had to pass calculus. She *had to.*

Chapter Eight

BEN

Ben rode to school thirty minutes early on Wednesday, sharing the bike path through the greenway with long-distance bikers and squirrels—kamikaze squirrels. He swore the little bastards jumped out in front of his bike on purpose. As if he wasn't wrecked enough this morning after staying up half the night worrying about the rent.

He was going to find Paige and tell her the original deal was off, and he wanted *thirty* dollars an hour to tutor her. That ought to take some of the pressure off Mom, and it wasn't like Paige was hard up for cash.

The bike rack was empty when he pulled into the parking lot. Then again, it never really filled up. Only a few freshmen bothered to ride, and who would if they had friends who drove Beemers? There weren't many of those in the lot yet, either.

He pushed his way through the main doors. The hallway crowd was pretty thin, but he bet Paige would be there already. She struck him as the type of girl who thought being five minutes early was the same as being late. The problem was he had no idea what rainbow she sat on before school. Her friends usually raced into class ten seconds before final bell, based on what he'd seen. But she was *always* in class before he was.

So where would a Type-A, overachieving princess hang out first thing in the morning?

He started with the library—nope. The cafeteria was always a total zoo and smelled like stale pizza, not her scene. He checked their AP English room, then Mr. Granger's classroom, to see if she had come in to meet with the teachers. She wasn't there, either.

Where could she be?

Out of ideas, he wandered down the music wing. Was she in choir? Band? She seemed like the choir type, but she wasn't in the choir room. He was about to leave when the sounds of classical piano caught his ear. Whoever was playing was incredible. He'd taken piano until he was eight, but after Dad left, Mom couldn't afford the lessons, so he quit. Still, he loved hearing a good person play.

He moved toward the sound, finding a little hallway behind an alcove at the back of the room. There were doors off each side of the hall—ah, practice rooms. There was a light on in the one at the very end, and Beethoven was pouring through the door. "Sonata in G Minor"? He'd just listened to it on the classical radio station while studying last weekend.

The music swelled and rolled through the allegro section. This was tough stuff, and the person playing was perfect, until the notes stumbled halfway through.

"Damn it!" a girl snapped. "Damn, damn, damn."

Ben grinned. He'd found his girl. Paige sure didn't like making mistakes, did she? He started for the door, thinking to surprise her, when the strains of "Demons" by Imagine Dragons came from her practice room. She really was good, improvising just enough to make the song more interesting without destroying the original melody. He leaned against the wall to listen. Her problem with the Beethoven seemed to be confidence, because she didn't miss a single note now. Or maybe something about this song spoke to her in a way the classical piece didn't.

Finally, when the last strain died away, he pushed himself off the wall and went to knock on the door…just as she flung it open.

She screeched and sheet music flew everywhere.

Ben's face flushed. He hadn't meant to scare her. "I seem to have a problem with catching you at bad moments, huh?"

"Were you…were you *listening*?" Her tone suggested that was a crime of terrible proportions. She dropped to her knees and began savagely rounding up her music.

She really needed to lighten up. "Yes. You're very good."

"Ha, hardly."

"Hey, it takes a long time to learn something as complex as the allegro." He bent to help her scoop up her music. "Quit being so hard on yourself. I wish I could play half that well."

She straightened up. "You play?"

"I did." He shrugged. "Had to quit, but I enjoy classical piano. Weird, I know."

"It's not weird," she said, looking wary. "It's just…"

"Weird," he said.

Paige smiled, and he noticed how it changed her whole face, like her stress had fallen away. "No, just different—and that's not the same as weird. Weird is someone who gets all baby-oiled up and worships a grand piano naked."

Ben burst out laughing. "For the record, I *don't* do that."

"Good, because then I'd have to run screaming." They stood and she asked, "Why are you here, though?"

"Um…" He paused, hoping she wouldn't ask him to explain why he'd changed his mind. "Look, about the Zoey thing…that was a really dumb favor for me to ask. The money would be good. I can use it for school."

Or rent, but whatever.

She frowned and led him out of the practice hall into the choir room. "Okay. If that's what you want."

Relief warred with the disappointment of a missed opportunity until his chest was tight with the conflict. "But, um, could we make it thirty an hour?"

They had moved out into the main hallway, but now she stopped by a bank of lockers in the science wing. "We can, but…is something going on? You were really excited about the makeover yesterday."

"I just need the cash," he said, a little more coldly than he'd planned.

Paige's frown softened. "Fine. Thirty it is."

He was surprised she'd agree so fast, but he decided not to say anything and ruin his luck, such that it was. They started walking toward AP English, and he found he didn't mind her company. She had more layers than he'd realized—she wasn't one of those one-dimensional popular girls, and that made her interesting. Tutoring her wouldn't be a total beating.

"Paige!" a sweet voice rang out. "I need to talk to you!"

It was Zoey, and she was headed straight for them. Like she was Moses, the sea of students parted without a ripple to let her by. She moved like the music Paige played, and more than one guy looked dazed as she passed.

A little core of hurt flared up in his heart. He'd come so close, but there wasn't anything he could do now. He and Mom needed a roof over their heads.

As Zoey came closer, he noticed Paige watching him. "Uh, what?" he asked.

She gave him a long look, and when Zoey paused a second to say hi to someone, she pulled him close to whisper, "It means a lot to you, doesn't it? Asking her out?"

Was he that bad at hiding his disappointment? "Yes, but I need the money more, so don't worry about it."

Zoey was on her way again, but Paige managed to say one more thing. "Fine, we'll split the difference. Fifteen an hour *and* I'll make you over. But I'd better make an A. Deal?"

He leaned back, stunned. He couldn't believe it—she was letting him have this deal both ways? "Why would you do that?"

"Because you seem like you deserve a break." Paige gave him a little shove toward class. "Go. We'll meet this evening and continue with the regular plan. Don't make me regret it."

He did as she asked, but it felt like he'd swallowed a live firecracker. He had no idea why she would help him, but he wouldn't question his luck. He glanced over his shoulder and saw Paige and Zoey with their heads together. Zoey was talking, smiling, laughing.

So was Paige…but when she caught him looking, she gave her head a little jerk, as if to say, *Get going!* He nodded, but he couldn't help noticing how *sad* she seemed. Her smile didn't reach her eyes, even if it was a good act. She was a pretty girl, despite looking sad. She wasn't as tall as Zoey, and almost delicate with her large brown eyes and curly brown hair. But she was far from delicate, wasn't she? There was a steel backbone under the cuteness. She looked so rundown and exhausted, though, that everything about her was muted, especially when she stood next to Zoey, who glowed like the sun.

He'd help Paige score that A and she'd feel better, right? And along the way, he'd show her how to be more chill about this stuff. She was like an overinflated tire—it could only perform so long before the pressure caused a catastrophic failure.

He smiled before ducking into English class. Good thing Paige knew a mechanic.

Chapter Nine

By the time school let out, Paige had had enough. She plowed through the crowded hallway, an arm wrapped around her middle. Ben had been so sweet about her awful piano playing this morning, *and* he'd given her the perfect opportunity to walk away from the Zoey plan. So what had she done? She'd offered to pay him while still helping him date her best friend. That logic was outer-space stupid, but the thought of letting him down had killed her. Now everything was grating on her nerves, especially Zoey.

Who also happened to be at her locker when Paige arrived. "Hey, glad I caught you!"

Was there time to drop through the floor and disappear? No? Sigh. "I have the ElderCare bake sale today, so I'm kind of in a rush."

"This won't take a minute. I know how you feel about

the center."

"Sorry. It's just…we planned this forever ago and I convinced Mom to skip her Junior League meeting to help, so I can't be late."

Zoey held up her hands. "Totally get it. No need to stress out Mrs. W., that's for damn sure. I know how she is. Anyway, I was just going to ask if you want to help me plan Senior Day?"

Paige rubbed at the ache in the back of her neck—yes, her schoolwork would be lighter next semester, but all the senior activities were going to take up her spare time. "When would we need to start?"

Zoey's shrug spoke volumes. "A few weeks? It takes a while to line up the carnival stuff."

Her best friend might be acting casual about this, but Paige knew how much it meant to Zoey. Senior Day was the last event before graduation, and it had to be perfect. Which meant you absolutely had to have Perfect Paige as your right-hand woman. "Okay. I…I can do it in a few weeks."

"You sure?"

"Yep."

Before Zoey could start planning—keeping her from the bake sale—Paige strode away as fast as her legs could take her. So what if she was only five-four, she could move when she needed to. And escaping was priority one right now, before she had a heart attack right here in the hall. She'd never live that down.

She took calming breaths all the way to her car. Maybe she should ask Ben to help with the Senior Day planning. If Zoey got to know him, surely she'd see he was a good guy. She might even relax the rules and date him. Especially after Paige fixed him up a little. Never mind that the idea of hooking up the two of them made her physically ill. Was she really that selfish? Why was doing the logical, kind thing for Ben making her feel so rotten?

But is it kind to ignore how you *feel?* a little voice whispered. *Maybe it's good for Zoey, but it won't be good for you.*

Since Paige couldn't figure out if it was the angel or the devil on her shoulder doing the talking, she couldn't trust it.

The drive to the ElderCare center cleared her head. She was at home here, which none of her friends could understand. Hang out with Alzheimer's patients? No way. Their loss, though, because her EC people were awesome, and another reason she decided to go into medicine.

The center wasn't like most nursing homes. It was less like a hospital and more like a big house. That's why Daddy sent his critical patients here—welcoming surroundings were less upsetting, and that was key for their treatment during his clinical trials. She'd started coming with him in eighth grade and felt at home as soon as she went into the rec room to play Go Fish with three of the residents. They made their own rules, then bickered about them, until Paige found a big poster board and wrote them out to stave off arguments. The nurses had asked how often she could come back to volunteer after that, and she came as often as she could.

Paige checked in at the front desk, then was buzzed through to the common room. As soon as she entered, a chorus of hellos rang out. Smiling, she went from person to person, passing out cookies, hugs, and compliments.

When she made it over to Mr. Kennedy, his eyes lit up.

"Don't tell me…don't tell me…Martha, is it you?"

Paige suppressed a giggle. She had no idea who Martha was, but Mr. Kennedy was a big fan, so she simply nodded. "Hello there."

"My dear, I was just telling Jack that we should set up a double date sometime."

Jack was his dead brother, but no matter how many times they told him, he'd forget, and making him suffer the grief of being told over and over was cruel. "That's very sweet of you, but I think Millie over there would be very jealous."

They turned to glance at Millie, who *was* giving them the evil eye. "Ah, guess you're right, Martha. It was worth a try."

She gave his hand a squeeze and went to pick up the desserts the nursing staff had made for the bake sale. There were storage containers and white bakery boxes lined up in the recreation office, covering the entire back counter.

"Whoa," Paige breathed, and a rush of gratitude filled her. They'd come through in a big way. She wished she'd asked her mom to help load everything instead of going straight to the library to set up, because it was obvious the staff cared as much about the patients as she did.

She loaded as much as she could carry, breathing in chocolate, cinnamon, and coconut with every step. By the time she finished filling up her car, she wanted to buy out the bake sale because it smelled so delicious and definitely *not* healthy.

When she arrived at the library, Mom's eyes bugged out at the sight of her full backseat. "What, did they rob Sunshine bakery?"

Paige laughed. "I'm just hoping we sell this stuff, because I want *all* the cakes."

Her mother frowned. "Honey, it's hardly healthy to want any of these cakes, let alone all of them. You know better."

Paige bit back a grimace, knowing that wasn't a surprising comment, considering the contents of their fridge. Tofu patties, anyone? "If we sell everything, I'll buy you an almond milk latte for helping."

"Big spender."

"I'd do better if you gave me more allowance." She batted her eyes, and Mom shook her head. "Okay, okay. But I do need some extra money."

"Oh? Is it for a school thing?"

Wasn't it? Or was it something else? Paige arranged a few cakes and a plate of brownies on the table, thinking about Ben's hopeful smile this morning, and straightened the plastic tablecloth before answering. "Yes...I, um, have a really great enrichment opportunity at school. It should enhance my math and, um...chemistry skills."

"I love how seriously you take your studies, honey. Dad and I were talking about that the other night. So many girls your age are completely boy crazy and don't care about school, but not our Paige. Hard work is a rewarding thing in the end. I've been saying it for years, and now you see it's true!" Mom opened her wallet. "How much do you need?"

She hid a cringe. She hated lying to her mom, but if she was going to make Ben over, she needed a bankroll. "Three hundred. It's an afterschool thing. That's why the fee's so high."

Mom shrugged and counted out the cash. "If it helps round out your premed portfolio, that's not too much to ask."

"Thanks," she said weakly, tucking the money into her

own purse.

"So, I've been meaning to ask—any progress up the class ladder?"

Paige kept her face turned away. "Still fourth. The competition is pretty tough. Samir is going to be valedictorian—he aced all the AP exams. There's no passing him."

"Are you sure, or do you just need to try harder?" Mom asked.

She forced herself to turn around and meet her mother's gaze. "I'm trying as hard as I can. Samir's a genius. Hard work is a good thing, like you said, but sometimes someone else has more talent."

"If that's how you feel about it, then that's that." Mom's lips pressed together. "Fourth is good enough for Stanford, I suppose."

But not for me—that was the unspoken addition to that sentence. Paige blinked fast against an attack of frustrated tears. "I'll see if there's any way to make up some ground."

"Good."

A harried mother holding hands with twin boys kept her from having to say any more. The little boys, who couldn't be more than five, practically dragged the woman up the sidewalk, shouting, "Cookies! Cookies, Mama!"

"It's almost dinner," the mom protested.

"But we want cookies!" one twin said, giving her a mischievous smile.

"Cookies will make us behave in the liberry," the other said.

She sighed and dug out her wallet. "How much for three of the chocolate-chocolate-chips?"

"Three dollars," Paige told her. "We're raising money for

the memory care center."

"Uh-huh." The mom was already distracted. She pulled out a five. "Good cause, keep the change."

The little family went to stand in the shade of one of the big live oaks surrounding the front of the Alderwood Library and inhaled their sweets. Mom shook her head. "Ruining their supper. I wish we'd tried to sell handmade jewelry or candles instead of junk food."

"People *like* junk food," Paige pointed out.

Mom pushed the low-fat brownies to the front of the table. "That doesn't make it responsible of us. We have to lead by example."

Responsible—something Paige had been her whole life, just like her mother. But now? Now she had bilked three hundred bucks off her mom to make over a boy so she could fix him up with her best friend. Maybe that word didn't mean exactly what she thought it did.

For the rest of the afternoon, Paige's brain wouldn't shut down. Thoughts about Ben, and lies, and Ds in calculus chased one another in a game of tag until she wanted to scream. The bake sale was slammed—despite Mom's objections, *lots* of people wanted to ruin their dinners—but as the clock rolled toward six, her mouth became dry and she paced behind the little table.

"Something wrong?" Mom asked.

"Huh? Uh, no. Nothing." Paige forced herself to stand still, fussing with the last few plates of dessert left. "I'm fine."

"You sure? You seem a little twitchy, honey."

Paige almost blurted out the whole thing, to relieve the pressure, but caught herself at the last second. "Oh, I'm just going over my piano piece in my head. Can never practice too much, right?"

The excuse satisfied Mom but did nothing to ease the ache behind Paige's breastbone. She was really doing this—Ben was going to come here, study with her, then she was going to take him out to the mall. Using Mom's money to do it. Even though the bake sale went great, raising almost four hundred dollars for the center, she couldn't enjoy it. She felt like such a fake, not telling Mom how she was failing calc.

For her parents, though, she had to be Perfect Paige. Even if she had to lie to do it.

Chapter Ten

BEN

Ben rode up to the library five minutes late, halfway expecting that Paige had changed her mind and found another tutor. But, no, her Mustang was in the parking lot. His stomach lurched. She'd lived up to her side of the bargain—so far—and here he was, late for their first session. Not exactly the best first impression.

He went inside, pausing to take a deep breath. He loved how the library smelled—paper, old books, and wood polish. Alderwood's library was in a historic building downtown, and a lot of its paneling and floors were original. He used to come here with his dad as a kid. They'd go to the children's section and pick out some books for him, then go over to the history section, where Ben would sit on the dusty wooden floor and read while his dad pulled down book after book, trying to decide what to read next.

Thinking about his dad usually made him feel a little pissed, but today he was just tired. Holding back a sigh at what might've been, he walked past the main circulation desk, through the mystery section, and by the computer bank to reach the study tables near the big windows at the back of the library. They overlooked the greenbelt, and slanted sunlight shone through the leaves outside, tinting Paige's brown hair a shining gold. She was hunched over a notebook with her calculus book open.

As he watched, she furiously erased something, then punched numbers into her graphing calculator. When she checked the result, she blew out an angry breath and tossed her pencil on the table.

And that's when he knew. She needed his help—*his* help, not someone else's.

He cleared his throat and she looked up. "Oh, you came."

"You thought I wouldn't?" he asked, settling down into the chair next to her. Like the floors and the walls, the table was solid wood, scuffed and worn from countless hours of studying.

"I wasn't sure," she murmured. "But I'm glad."

In spite of everything, he smiled. "So, want to tell me why you tried to kill your calculator with blunt force a second ago?"

"Critical points. I can't get this." The look she turned on him was so bleak he actually felt scared for her. "I'm so stupid."

"Whoa, whoa, whoa," he protested. "You're fourth in our class. Fourth, Paige. You are *not* stupid."

"I won't be fourth after Mr. Granger enters my test score into the grading system."

"We'll get you back there." He laughed. "I would offer to help you make it to third, but that's me, and I'm kind of competitive."

A little smile twitched at the corner of her mouth. "No ladies first on that one?"

"Nope." Good, she was still smiling, and he smiled, too. "So, can I take a look at your work?"

She nodded and they dived in. The longer they studied, the more Ben realized Paige's problem really was stress. She didn't believe she could do it, so even when she was doing a problem correctly, she second-guessed herself and changed it to something wrong.

"Listen," he said after an hour. "I think I know how to fix this, but I also think you need a break. I'm almost afraid to ask, but weren't we going to do 'phase one' of your plan tonight?"

Paige looked up from her book, startled, then looked out the window. It was almost sunset, and the sky was streaked with pink and orange. "I didn't notice what time it was." She smiled shyly. "You're a good teacher."

For some reason, that vulnerable little smile and the praise made him flush all over. "Thanks. And you can do this, okay?"

"Okay." She stood and started packing up her books. "We need to hurry to the mall before it closes."

He tensed up. The mall? "Why? What's at the mall?"

"Phase one. Now, come on." She led him through the library. "The less I tell you, the more likely I'll get my way."

"Do you always get your way?" he asked, trotting along behind her.

"Yep."

"I was afraid of that."

They made it to the parking lot, and Paige looked around. "Did you drive here?"

Now he flushed for an entirely different reason. "No. I rode my bike."

"Oh. Do you want to put it in my car?"

There was no way it would fit in her tiny Mustang. "You know what, just bring me back here after, and I'll ride home."

She turned to frown at him. "But it'll be late. How far are you going? I could drive you."

"No," he said quickly. No way was he letting her see his house. "It's not far. It'll be fine."

She didn't look convinced, but she didn't ask, either. "Okay, then let's go."

They rode to the mall mostly in silence, but it wasn't weird. The radio played in the background and he found it cute that Paige hummed along without seeming to notice. She was a good driver, too, hopping onto George Bush Expressway without flinching. She moved confidently around traffic, like she did this all the time. He'd expected her to be one of those white-knuckled drivers, avoiding the highway at all costs.

Paige Westfield definitely wasn't who he'd assumed.

"Where are we going?" he asked as she parked at the south end of the mall.

"Not telling."

Now *that* was the Paige he expected.

She dragged him past Hollister and a host of other stores. "Ah, here we are. And right on time."

"A salon?" he yelped. When she shot him an amused—and triumphant—glance, he cleared his throat. "I'm getting a haircut?"

"Oh, not a haircut. A hair*style*."

"There's a difference?"

She rolled her eyes and pushed him into the salon. A slender man with purple streaks in his black hair came hurrying out. "Paigey-Paige!"

"Hey, Joey!"

They hugged and Ben took a step back, hoping he'd melt into the wall. No such luck. Joey released Paige, looking him over. "I see what you mean, girl. Who cut your hair, honey? Edward Scissorhands?"

He scowled. "I used a lawnmower."

"Ben," Paige hissed, but Joey laughed.

"Oh, I like him. He has some sass. Come on back, Lawnmower Head. We have work to do."

Joey disappeared behind a partition separating the front of the salon from the back. Ben shot a helpless look at Paige, who waved her fingers at him, giggling. "You two have fun. I'll be back in half an hour to check in."

"You're *leaving* me?"

"Joey's a pro. You'll be fine."

Ben sucked down a panicked breath. He hadn't been this freaked out since he'd dropped a tire on Juan's toe by accident. "His. Hair. Is. Purple."

"And it looks great on him. Don't worry, you'll love Joey." She held up a hand. "Wait, what size pants do you wear?"

Bewildered, he blurted out, "Thirty-two waist, thirty-four length. Why?"

"Thanks. See you later." She turned and walked out, leaving him alone in the front of the salon.

"Hey, Lawnmower!" Joey shouted from somewhere behind the partition. "Water's hot. Let's rock and roll."

Chapter Eleven

Paige was still giggling when she went into Gap. She'd decided to avoid trendier stores because they were on a budget, and because she didn't think Ben would be comfortable in clothes that weren't classic or old school. Besides, she only had twenty-five minutes or so, which limited her options.

What she didn't realize was how fun it was to shop for a guy. Especially someone who was a blank canvas. If Zoey didn't appreciate the effort after she'd dressed Ben up, well, she was blind.

When she took the clothes to the register, the sales girl nodded in appreciation. "Good mix and match options. You can make at least five outfits out of this."

Paige guessed she could make seven or eight after she raided Daddy's closet. He had a ton of great sweaters and button-downs from J. Crew that he never wore and probably didn't even know were in there. She smiled—Ben was going to look better than Jace by the time she was done. Being a perfectionist had some perks after all.

"What about shoes?" the sales girl asked. "The boyfriend will look great, but he needs shoes."

"He's not my boyfriend," she blurted. But her cheeks grew warm, and she couldn't keep from wondering how Ben's hair was shaping up. That was normal, right? He was an experiment, wasn't he? "He's just a friend-friend."

"Uh-huh. Just a friend." The clerk smirked a little as she folded all the clothes and slid them into a plastic shopping bag. "Your 'friend' will need some shoes, maybe a pair of kickass boots. Doc Martens or something like it."

Ouch, that would be expensive. She was already two hundred dollars into this project, and there was no way she could stretch her cash that far. And would Ben even wear something like that? Well, all she could do was ask, right?

She gathered up her bags, said thanks, then walked back to the salon. When she went inside, the first thing she heard was laughter.

The second thing was Ben wailing, "But…but…how?"

"It's not that tough, honey," Joey said.

Definitely curious, she went around the partition…and dropped her shopping bags on the floor. "Oh my God. You look…"

"Stupid?" Ben supplied.

"Um, no. No, the word I was looking for was *amazing*."

And he *did* look amazing. Gone was the uneven, slightly shaggy cut. Joey had trimmed most of his hair down close, but left the top long enough to be spiked and messy. You could actually see his face now, the sharp angles of his jawline, and the way his cheekbones tilted upward just a little.

Her stomach fluttered—she'd been wrong. Ben Franklin wasn't cute. He was gorgeous.

"Uh-huh, *amazing*'s the word, because I'm an artist," Joey said, wagging a pair of scissors at Ben. Neither of them seemed to notice that her knees were knocking together. "He's worried about the gel procedure."

Paige choked out a laugh. "Do I even want to ask?"

"No!" Ben said, right as Joey said, "Styling, and it's not that hard."

Ben sighed. "Fine."

"We'll buy some gel, then," she told them. A grin stretched across her face. He looked so *good*. More adult than most of the guys at school, for sure, which was definitely a Zoey requirement.

Ben was eyeing the bags. "What's in those?"

"Your new wardrobe. By the way, Joey?" She opened a bag and tipped it toward him. "The girl I shopped with said boots, but that seems too—"

"Industrial," Joey said. "High-top Converse. Black. Quirky but traditional. Suits him, you think?"

"Yes! Perfect." Converse were sixty dollars. This was doable, and he'd look great. Maybe *too* great.

Ben was watching the exchange like he was at a tennis match. His eyes went back and forth, back and forth, before he covered his face with his hands. "I think school is going to suck tomorrow."

"Oh, where's your sense of adventure?" She bit her lip, still smiling. "But remember, you asked for this."

"I did?"

"Yes. Now come on, we have one more stop to make."

Ben stood, quietly thanked Joey, and followed her out of the store. He was walking so close to her that their arms brushed, and they leapt apart like he'd shocked her. He gave her a startled, almost shy look. "Sorry. I didn't mean to… Um, shoes?"

Feeling a blush creep from her cheeks all the way down to her toes, Paige nodded. "Shoes."

Chapter Twelve

BEN

Ben watched the lights stream by on the highway. Paige had offered to drive him home, given the huge bags of clothes she'd bought for him, and he couldn't decide what to do. On the one hand, riding home with the clothes crammed into his backpack wouldn't be easy. On the other, leaving his bike at the library overnight was begging for it to be stolen. But that wasn't the whole reason…

He *really* didn't want Paige to see his house.

"So where should I exit?" Paige asked. She still had that triumphant little smile on her face.

His hands clenched in his lap. It didn't matter what he decided—either option would lead to embarrassing questions. Still, the thought of her in his house… "Um, just head to the library. I shouldn't leave my bike there."

She was quiet a moment, then held up a finger. "Let's go

to my house. My mom has an Escalade. I can switch cars, and we'll be able to pick up your bike. It'd be too much to try to ride with all this stuff."

Misery twisted in Ben's stomach. An Escalade…and she said it like it was no big deal. Then again, a big-ass Cadillac probably *wasn't* a huge deal to her. "It's fine. Really. If you'll just hang onto the shoes, I can…I can pick them up tomorrow."

"Are you wimping out on me?" she asked, looking worried. "Or is it your hair? Oh, my hell, do you hate your hair? I should've asked first, I know, but—"

"No." He laughed a little. Insecurity was going to kill this experiment, one way or another, before it even started. Which one of them would cave first? "As much as I hate to admit it, I kind of like my hair."

"Really?"

She sounded so relieved. Pleased, even, like this admission made her night. "Really."

She didn't say anything for a while, and Ben spent some time arguing with himself about doing the logical thing and letting her drive him home, or maintaining a little pride and making it on his own. They pulled off the highway, and when she took the turn toward the library, he hoped it meant she was deciding for him.

"Ben?" she asked softly.

"Yeah?"

"I, um, I won't judge your house. I mean, if that's what's bothering you."

They stopped at a red light and he turned to look at her. She kept her eyes focused straight ahead on the road. Her expression was kind, but it wasn't that "rich kid pity" he'd had thrown in his face over and over. No, this was something else. She really wanted him to feel comfortable. The light turned green, but Paige didn't go. The road was deserted, and she seemed to be waiting for instructions.

He looked down the street to their right. The library was only a few blocks away. He had no idea where she lived. Probably in a huge, immaculate house with expensive furniture and a big, spiraling staircase.

His shoulders slumped. His pride was getting the better of him. Again. Maybe he should accept the offer and stop being judgmental of *her*.

"You're different than I expected," he said.

"What did you expect?" She wouldn't look at him, but her tone was shy.

Something was happening, and he couldn't be sure what. It was like that moment his arm had touched hers at the mall—the only word in his head had been *electric*. She'd seemed as stunned by it as he had. "I don't know."

"That's okay. You're different than I expected, too," she murmured. "So, which way should I go?"

He'd followed her willingly—not entirely trusting, but whatever, it had worked out okay—all night. He didn't know what it was about Paige Westfield that had suddenly lit all his nerve endings on fire, but he believed her when she said she wouldn't judge.

A car pulled onto the street behind them, so he drew a deep breath and said, "Can we go get your mom's car? I think you're right…that would be easier."

She nodded, and he caught the flicker of a smile before she turned left. Now that he'd agreed, nerves set in, and he had to wipe his hands on his jeans more than once as she drove him through nice neighborhoods to Alderwood Hills—home of Alderwood Country Club and the highest concentration of millionaires in North Texas. They turned onto a street lined with McMansion after McMansion. The streetlights were so well kept and bright that he could tell every lawn was like carpet and the trees were imported for size, because the subdivision was too new to have fifty-year-old oaks and elms like these.

At Morganville Road, Paige turned right. The houses on this street weren't quite as big as some of the others, but they were still really nice, all of them two stories with the same big lawns and old trees.

"Here we are." She pulled into the driveway of a white colonial-style house surrounded by live oaks. "Want to come in? I need Mom's keys."

He stared at the big, well-lit porch, lined with white rocking chairs and potted plants. "Um…I can wait out here. It's okay."

Paige laid a hand on his arm and he jumped, just like at the mall. Her skin was warm on his. "She doesn't bite. Promise."

He couldn't think. Why couldn't he think while she touched him? And he'd become aware of her perfume. It had surrounded him in the car for miles, but he'd just noticed it. Something light and floral. Not overpowering, but it had his full attention now.

"Ben?"

She had a worried look on her face. It took all his concentration to nod and reach for his door handle. The fresh air helped. What was going on with him?

Paige was already halfway to the front door. "You

coming?"

"Uh, yeah." He trotted up the walk to meet her, then followed her inside. The entryway was enough to make him stop cold and gape. Hardwood floors the color of honey gleamed in all directions, and the curved staircase he'd expected led up to a second floor. Original paintings hung on the walls, too. Plus he didn't see a single nick in the paint. What, didn't they ever accidentally lose hold of the door and bang the knob into the sheetrock?

"Mom!" Paige called. "I need your car!"

A muffled "Why?" came from somewhere in the back of the house. Which, to his estimation, was two miles from where they stood. He shuffled his feet, wishing they could just go. God, this was a big house, and it wasn't even that big compared to the rest of the neighborhood. What was she going to think of his place? He bet her bedroom was the size of his whole house.

"Need to drive a friend home. We have parts of a science project that are too big for my car."

He had to hand it to her, she could lie with ease. He hadn't thought she had it in her, but there was a little bit of truth embedded in the "science project" story, so maybe she justified the lie that way.

There was a long pause, then heels clicked on the wood. A pretty woman who looked a lot like Paige—petite and brown-eyed, except with lighter hair—came around a corner through the sitting room. Even though it was late, she was dressed in nice pants, a crisply ironed shirt, and heels. Makeup done and everything.

Mrs. Westfield looked surprised to see that the "friend" was a guy, and he could practically feel her weighing and measuring him with her stare alone. Based on the pinched skin between her eyes and the tiny wrinkle to her nose, she'd found him wanting. He hunched his shoulders and shoved his hands in his pockets, wishing he'd told Paige to leave him at the library.

Paige's mom seemed to realize, too late, that she was being kind of rude, because when Paige said, "This is Ben," in a tone that clearly told her mom to play nice, her expression shifted into a polite smile.

"Nice to meet you, Ben." Her tone suggested it wasn't *all* that nice, and he flushed. She held up a set of car keys. "How long will you be? I don't like you out after dark."

Paige rolled her eyes. "I'll be back in less than an hour. Promise."

Mrs. Westfield leveled a cool stare his way. "I'll expect you then. Be careful."

Don't trust the poor boy hung unspoken in the air, and Ben's embarrassed flush intensified, except now he was fuming. He dug his hands deeper into his pockets, wanting to say, *Look, I can't steal anything if my hands aren't free*, to see what Mrs. Westfield would do.

If Paige noticed anything was wrong, she was much better at hiding her feelings than her mom. "I always am."

She grabbed the keys, then stalked down the hallway leading deeper into the house. Helpless, Ben followed, passing a wood-paneled office with a desk overflowing with file folders, a living room the size of a small movie theater, and a ginormous, gleaming kitchen that looked like it belonged in a restaurant, not a house.

They ended up in a four-car garage. Next to a black Escalade was a red 1960s Stingray Corvette. "Wow."

Paige threw it a glance. "Meh. Dad's midlife crisis car. He only drives it on sunny weekends. Most of the time he takes the Audi."

Obviously Dr. Westfield took the Audi. Why wouldn't he? Ben's palms started to sweat again. Would he ever be comfortable in a place like this?

She opened the garage door, then climbed into the Escalade. "You ready?"

He looked at the immaculate garage with its gleaming cars and lack of oil stains, and his spirits sank. How could she *not* judge his house? "Yeah."

Chapter Thirteen

PAIGE

God, Paige could just kill her mother. Where had that snooty, country-club attitude come from? Or was the nasty face because she'd brought a boy to the house right after Mom had given her the old "I'm so glad you aren't like other girls" speech? Either way, Mom had made Ben feel like an intruder when he was supposed to be a guest.

Guh.

Now poor Ben was sitting stiff and still in the passenger seat of the Escalade, like the leather was going to scald him. She didn't miss the hurt, fear, and confusion in his eyes, either. Her heart ached for him. Had she been stupid to want to take him home so he didn't have to ride so far?

"You can turn on the radio," she said. "I'll listen to whatever."

He shot her a sideways glance, then leaned forward and

turned on the satellite radio function. Mom had left it set to the eighties station, and "With or Without You" was on. His hand hovered over the buttons. "You like this one?"

"Yeah," she said, turning in to the library's parking lot. "Mom makes me listen to old stuff all the time. U2's fine."

It took only a minute to load his bike into the back— Ben doing most of the work, which seemed to lighten his mood a little. When they got back into the car, the tension settled around her like a wool blanket. And it was too damn humid for wool.

"If you don't want me to drive you home, it's fine. Really."

"No, how else are we going to take everything there?" He stared at his hands. "I don't suppose you'll tell me how much all this cost?"

"Not nearly enough if I make an A in calc," Paige said with a smile before pulling out onto Main. "Now, where to?"

Sighing, he gave her directions to an old neighborhood on the south side of town. "Wait, how far do you ride every day?"

"Five miles, just to school. Probably fifteen or twenty most days."

Twenty miles, and he said it like it was no big deal. "But… can't you ride the bus?"

He laughed. "Would *you* ride the bus with a bunch of freshmen?"

"No." She was afraid to ask him if he'd let her drive him to school. That could be a battle for another day. Tonight it was enough that he trusted her with his address, and she was pleased he trusted her that much. "A bus full of freshmen would be enough to get *me* to ride a bike twenty miles."

He laughed. "I'd pay half my savings to see that."

"If it weren't so late, I'd take your bike for a spin for nothing but a chance to make you laugh again," she said.

"You would?" he asked softly, and when she turned, he was smiling—this sweet, genuine smile that made her want to trace his mouth with a fingertip.

She cleared her throat. "Yeah. Sure."

When they drove up his street, Ben shifted uncomfortably. The neighborhood was really dark—no streetlights, and half the houses didn't have exterior lighting. Not even porch lights. Of what she *could* see, the houses were small but neatly kept, with tidy little lawns. Oh, there were a few with rusted-out cars in the driveways, but those were the exception. It wasn't nearly as bad as he seemed to think it was.

"Here," he said, pointing to a house with siding that glowed yellow in her headlights. She turned in to the drive-way, stopping short of the carport, because she wasn't sure the Escalade would fit under the canopy, and how would that be? Oh—thanks for showing me your home. Here, let me destroy part of it for you.

Ben hopped out and unloaded his bike, and she waited, unsure. She wanted him to ask her in, but she was scared she'd spook him if she mentioned it. Instead, she turned off the car and pulled out the shopping bags.

When he came back, she handed them to him. "We can start phase two this weekend if you want."

"Um, okay. I'm only off Saturday morning and Sunday."

She wrapped her arms around herself. Just how much did he have to work? It was so unfair, but it didn't seem to bother him. He was kicking school's ass like a boss while working crazy hours, and she was flunking calculus. Ben Franklin was a freaking ninja compared to her.

He was looking at her like he was waiting for her to say something. "Yeah, Saturday morning would work."

Ben rocked from foot to foot, then said, "Want to come in? I mean, it's not much, but—"

"I'd love to!" she answered in a rush, before he could change his mind. He raised an eyebrow and Paige almost laughed—he and Zoey could play Eyebrow Battle Royale when they went out. A wave of cold washed over her. She had to stop thinking about how this would all end, otherwise she'd make herself sick. "Well, are we going in or not?"

Looking nervous, he let her in a side door near the carport. The first thing she noticed was the house smelled like... "Brownies? You have brownies? For real? Where are they? Can I have some?"

He hung his keys on a hook by the door and turned to her, smiling. "My mom usually cooks stuff before she goes to work. We can go look."

They went through a tiny utility room—more like a hallway—into a small, clean kitchen. The rest of the room, because it was all one room, had a little dining table and a living area with a sofa and a TV. Paige took all that in with one quick glance, then zeroed in on the baking pan on the range. Speechless, she merely pointed and gave Ben a single, pleading look.

By now he was laughing. "If I'd known you had a brownie fetish, I wouldn't have worried so much about bringing you home."

He pulled the foil off the pan and cut her a big square. The first bite was heaven. "Ohhhh my God. Mmmm."

"Okay, so *fetish* was the right word. You sound a little like a porn soundtrack." He cut a brownie for himself. "What, you don't eat brownies at your house?"

"No." She had to eat another bite before explaining further. Heavenly bliss on a napkin. "My mother, in addition to being randomly rude—I'm so sorry for the way she acted, by the way, because she was a total bitch. No idea what her problem was. Anyway, she's a health fiend, and an all-organic champion. No junk food is allowed in the house. When Mom bakes, it's low-fat, gluten-free, and non-GMO. She wouldn't even let me buy something good at my own bake sale today. I have to buy candy bars on the way to school and hoard them in my locker if I want a fix."

"Wow…that sucks," he said emphatically before popping the rest of his brownie in his mouth.

She nodded, too drunk on chocolate to bother answering.

His expression softened, and he reached out to brush her cheek. Goose bumps covered her arms and she gulped down her brownie. "What is it?"

He leaned forward, looking down into her eyes, before smiling. "Crumb on your cheek."

She flushed head to toe, not sure if she was embarrassed or something else. Good God, she needed some air. Their faces were inches apart. All she'd have to do was lean forward and tilt her mouth up and they'd kiss. Would that bother him? Scare him off? He swayed closer to her and his hand drifted from her face to her shoulder.

No, to hell with worrying about it. She *wanted* him to kiss her. She turned her face up to his, and their lips were a breath away from touching. He stared down at her, mouth slightly open, and any second now, any second and he would kiss her. Any second…

Her phone buzzed in her purse.

Ben jumped, then took a step back. "Thanks for taking me shopping tonight. I had fun."

Somehow, she croaked out, "Good," even though she was shaking. And disappointed. And relieved.

But mostly disappointed.

He pointed to the brownie pan. "One for the road?"

"Yes, please." While he was dishing out two big brownies and wrapping them in paper towels, she looked around at his house a little more. There was a door at the back of the living room that probably led to the bedrooms. She didn't know why he was so embarrassed. Everything was spotless. So what if their TV was an older model and the carpet was a little worn? "I like your house. It looks…homey."

He handed her the package of brownies. "Is that a nice way of saying it looks rundown?"

"No," she murmured. "It's a nice way of saying that whoever lives here is loved."

"It's not so bad." He looked around the room like he'd never seen it before. "Anyway, what about these clothes? What do I do with them?"

"Wear them, I hope."

Ben smiled. "Yes, I know. But…what goes with what? And, um, do I wear them to school, or… Look, I'm a T-shirt and jeans kind of guy. I don't know anything about this stuff."

"Have you even looked in the bags?" Paige asked.

He opened the first one. "Yes."

"Good grief. Okay, so, yes, you wear them to school. There are two pairs of jeans, one pair of chinos, and one pair of cords, for when it's cooler. There are a few T-shirts, some button-downs, and a cool jacket I liked. Wear the blue striped T-shirt and the dark jeans tomorrow."

"Got it," he said, pulling out the cords. "These are nice."

"Thanks. I have good taste."

"Yeah…about that. I don't know if I can repay you for all this."

"You don't have to," she said. "It's half of your tutoring fee."

"So am I tutoring you for twenty hours?" he asked.

She wished. Hoped. "I'm pretty bad at calc."

"You're not. You're just worrying too much." He set the bag down and gripped her arms. She barely repressed a shiver as his eyes pinned her in place. "You're brilliant, Paige Westfield. Stop beating yourself up all the time, or…or…"

"Or what?" she whispered.

He smiled slowly and chills raced down her spine. "Or I'll mismatch all these clothes and tell everyone at school you picked out my outfit."

Her brain was going to explode from all these mixed signals pretty soon. "You wouldn't."

"I might." They stared at each other a moment too long, a heartbeat past what just friends would do. Then Ben abruptly let her go. "Promise me, though. Promise you'll start paying attention to how amazing you are."

But not as amazing as Zoey, apparently. Paige doubted he would've gone to such lengths to win *her* over, and that sucked. Why couldn't *she* be the "one" this time? "I promise."

Suddenly exhausted and more than a little sad, she left before he could say anything else.

Chapter Fourteen

BEN

Ben leaned against the kitchen counter for a long time after Paige left. He'd been so sure she would've turned her nose up at his house, at *him*, but she hadn't. She'd been eager to look around and hadn't once said anything snobby. The weird thing? She'd seemed happier here than at her place. She had that huge house, but it seemed so empty. Her mom acted like she was more interested in making her into this clean-eating, super student than loving Paige for who she was.

Which was so stupid, because she was incredible.

And what about that moment when he'd brushed the crumb from her cheek? Or when he was holding her arms, telling her to believe in herself? He'd felt something shift between them, but he wasn't sure if he was imagining it. The way she'd held his eyes, and how her breath had mingled with his…it had seemed like she was *interested*. For about three seconds they'd been staring at each other and he'd had this crazy longing to kiss her. Wanting to find out how her lips would feel against his. Would she feel small in his arms? Or just right? Would she kiss him back?

He snorted. Definitely his imagination. This wasn't like summer Robotics camp in Austin last year, with every girl looking to hook up with a hot nerd—he'd been the Jace Tillman of that crowd and had played it to his advantage. He'd had more action in those three weeks than in the last three years of high school. This thing with Paige was different, though. Thank God her phone had interrupted them, because she would've smacked him if he'd tried anything. Like Zoey, she was out of his league.

Which was too bad, because the thought of kissing her was far from terrible. In fact, it would probably be pretty wonderful.

Whoa, where did *that* come from? Paige was only helping him because she needed a tutor. If she hadn't been so desperate, she probably wouldn't have given him a second look. It was great they worked so well together, but thoughts of kissing needed to be shoved aside. They had an arrangement. He had to remember that and focus on the goal: Paige needed that A in calc, and he would like more than a passing glance from Zoey.

So why did it feel wrong? Zoey was who he wanted… right?

Right?

No, don't even think about that. Paige's mom had looked at him like something scraped off the bottom of a mechanic's shoe. Being friends with her at school would have to be enough—he had the feeling he wouldn't be welcome at the Westfields' castle anytime soon.

Wait, would that be a problem for Zoey, too? He wasn't sure. Damn it, he hated being so unsure all the time. Why couldn't he be comfortable in his own skin? Why couldn't plain Ben Franklin be enough? Was that why he'd set his sights on Zoey? She was the most unattainable girl at Alderwood, and if he went out with her, that would prove that he was someone special, and not just a mechanic, written off by everyone at school.

Funny thing, though, Paige had never once looked at him like that. Zoey might be the same way. Maybe it wouldn't matter who he was right now. All he needed was for Zoey to see his potential.

Like Paige did.

God, why was everything so confusing all of a sudden? He had a plan, both for the next few weeks and the next ten years. *Stick to the plan, Ben. Stick. To. The. Plan.*

He took the shopping bags to his room and spread everything out on his bed, stopping when he caught his reflection in the mirror. He hadn't had hair this short since sixth grade. This was going to take some getting used to. But— more than he'd ever admit to Paige—he really liked it. The spiky top made him look older, like he was already in college and moving on with his life. He glanced at the dark jeans and the blue and white T-shirt. The clothes looked "college guy," too. Maybe it was time to try his future life on for size, and see if it fit.

He hung up the clothes, smiling. He'd have to work really hard to help Paige to feel like he could pay her back for this, but it might just be worth it.

When he finally went to sleep that night, long before his mom made it home from the late shift, the last image he had was Paige's face, watching him as they nearly kissed.

He wished he'd kissed her…even if he was sure she would've smacked him. It would've been worth it.

Chapter Fifteen

"I'm home!" Paige shouted in the general vicinity of her parents' room as she hustled through the kitchen on her way to the back set of stairs. She wasn't in the mood to make an appearance, and she was so pissed at Mom it didn't seem like a good idea to try.

Besides, her heart was still lurching after what had happened in Ben's kitchen. She was so sure he'd been about to kiss her, and what happened? Mom texted to remind her to come on home, like she was twelve. What would've happened if she hadn't been interrupted? Would Ben have kissed her? And if he had, then what? A secret part of her heart—the frustrated part—had a momentary hope he would've seen her for real and forgotten Zoey even existed. That, just once, the guy would've picked *her*.

Whether that would've happened or not, she was so

damn *annoyed* her mom had broken the spell she wanted to cry. Okay, it wasn't totally Mom's fault. She was so tired, and the stress of hiding her calc grade was getting to her, too. Her parents would freak when they found out, and it was making her stomach hurt. Those brownies sat like a rock in her stomach. God, when had her life gotten so…messy?

"Sweet Pea?"

She held in a groan, barely. "Hi, Daddy."

He came in from his den and gave her a quick hug. "How was your day?"

How did she even answer that? "Okay, I guess."

"So Mom says you were with a boy tonight." His brows knitted together. "Anybody I need to meet? Maybe while I'm cleaning my shotgun?"

In spite of herself, she smiled. "You don't have a shotgun."

"I could, though. We're in Texas. I could have shotguns if I wanted to." He kissed her forehead. "So who is he, this mystery boy?"

"His name is Ben. He's a…study partner. That's all." *Unfortunately.* "He's really nice, no matter what Mom told you."

Her tone came across defensive, and Daddy nodded slowly. "She was a little unhappy that you were traipsing around after dark, especially with a boy we hadn't met."

Why were they always smothering her with concern? Hadn't she shown them they could trust her yet? "Ben's a perfectly respectable guy, not some drug dealer from south Dallas."

"Hey now, I don't think she meant anything by it. I think she was just feeling overprotective."

Story of her whole life. "Can I go to my room now? I still

have homework to do."

"You said you and this Ben were studying. Why would you still have homework?"

"He's not *this Ben.*" She rubbed her eyes, wishing she could go straight to bed. What was with the interrogation? Riding around town with a guy wasn't so terrible. They wanted her to be perfect, but in the way they expected, not by her own standards. "And we did study. But I have more homework. Honors classes aren't a walk in the park."

"Why are you upset?" Daddy asked, looking baffled. "We just want to know who the kid is."

"A friend, Daddy. That's all." She brushed past him. "I'll be in my room."

She left him spluttering in the kitchen, nearly colliding with her mom as she rounded the corner. She pushed past without saying anything, then stomped up the stairs to her bedroom. She needed…something. A kiss? A nap? More brownies? No, the brownies were safely stowed in her car for eating tomorrow at school, and she definitely wasn't hungry.

She sank down on her bed. She should be feeling better—she'd successfully made over Ben, and her calculus homework was making a little sense to her now. So why was everything so screwed up?

Her phone buzzed. It was Zoey

Z: *What was the reading for government?*

Paige sighed. Zoey never wrote down the assignments, always expecting her to help. *Ch. 7. Quiz tmo. Study.*

Z: *I am, jeez. How was the bake sale?*

P: *Awesome. I'm really tired, tho.*

Z: *You've looked tired for a while, girl. I'm worried about you. How bout this—I'll study, you sleep. Bye!*

Paige shoved her phone under her pillow. Zoey was right—she needed to sleep. Maybe she'd do her homework in the morning before school.

Maybe she wouldn't do it at all.

That thought stuck for a moment, giving her a feeling somewhere between freedom and soul-crushing guilt. No, she'd do it, because that's what she always did—Perfect Paige, living up to everyone else's standards.

But Ben was different. He'd told her she was amazing. No one had ever said that before. Oh, they'd said "conscientious" or "driven" or "intelligent." But not *amazing*. That one word hung on her heart like a talisman. What did he see in her that no one else did? And why couldn't he see she was the right girl for him, not Zoey? If the two of them became a couple, would she be able to stand it? Could she plaster a fake smile on her face day after day, watching them be happy, while she was alone? The very idea made those brownies threaten to make a return visit.

Her limbs were heavy as she hauled herself up to change into PJs and get ready for bed. Luckily, her room had a door straight into her bathroom, so she didn't have to appear in the hall in case her parents were watching for her. For the rest of the night, she just wanted to curl up around that single word from Ben, and sleep without worry.

It must've worked, because sun was shining through the window Thursday morning when her phone buzzed her awake from under the pillow. In a panic, she checked the clock. It was early, right before her alarm was due to go off. Who was texting so early?

She checked the phone and her heart stuttered. It was Ben.

And when she saw the message, she started laughing.

Chapter Sixteen

Ben

Ben stared at his phone, waiting for an answer. His text, *So how do I fix my hair again?*—which included a picture—was probably being read with a ton of giggles, but his head looked like a hedgehog had sat on it and he needed the help.

P: *Gel, goofball. Joey showed you how, remember?*

B: *Sigh. Okay, I was hoping the gel was a lie.*

P: *No, the cake is a lie. The gel is God's own truth. So use it.*

Ben sat back and grinned at the screen. *The cake is a lie?* How in the world did Paige know about *Portal?* Layers…the girl had layers. He almost texted *It was a triumph* back, but realized that might be *too* dorky for seven a.m.

B: *Thanks. I'll use the gel. See you at school. No laughing at my hair.*

P: *Too late. Nice picture by the way. I should make it the lock screen on my phone.*

B: *Please don't.*

P: *Bye, Ben. Remember—blue T-shirt, dark jeans.*

B: *Yes, ma'am.*

He shoved his phone into the pocket of his new jeans—the dark ones, as instructed—and spent ten minutes trying to make his hair look something like it had last night. Then he realized he had a problem. Between his bike helmet, the wind, and the sweaty five-mile ride, the spikes were going to last about thirty seconds.

Sighing, he shoved the tube of gel into his backpack. Paige could fix him up at school.

On his way out, he stopped to grab a granola bar. Even though he was trying to be super quiet, Mom shuffled into the kitchen before he had a chance to leave. She was wearing her pink robe with the cats on it, and her dark hair stuck out in all directions. Now that he had short hair, he could appreciate bedhead on a whole new level. But what concerned him more was how thin she looked. When she worked a lot of hours, she didn't have enough time to eat much on her breaks, which made him feel guilty about the dinners and treats she always left behind for him.

"Morning," she said, opening the cabinet to take down the jar of instant coffee. Her yawn was huge, and there were dark circles under her eyes.

"When did you come home last night?" he asked. "You have to work late?"

She nodded. "I stayed until close, and there was a private party. They stayed until nearly one, but the tips were good." After putting on the kettle, she turned to him, frowning. "Where'd the clothes come from? I haven't seen those. And...did you cut your hair?"

Ben's brain locked up. She probably wouldn't like hearing a rich girl from the Club side had bought them for him. "Um..."

"Benjamin Fisher Franklin, where did you get those clothes?" she asked, hands on her hips.

Uh-oh, she was giving him the full-on treatment. And, as if it wasn't bad enough his name was Ben Franklin, his initials were "BFF." His mother had been on serious drugs when she filled out his birth certificate, which was why he *never* told anyone his middle name.

His shoulders drew up around his ears. If he was this self-conscious about how he looked around his mom, how was school going to be? "I'm tutoring someone for some extra money, so I bought a few things and got a haircut. You know, in case I need to meet with college recruiters," he said, almost wincing at the lie. "I know we need the rent money, but—"

Her hands came off her hips and she smiled tiredly. "Honey, you let me worry about the rent, okay? You deserve to spend your earnings on nice things every once in a while. I just wondered if your dad had sent you some money."

A hard core of anger flared in his chest at the mention of Dad. "Yeah, as if. I haven't seen a dime since he left, and neither have you."

"True, but stranger things have happened. That would be a better and more likely story than you dealing meth, right?"

Ben snorted. "I may be good at science, but I'm not Walter White, Ma. I need to go or I'll be late. Oh, and I'm working at the garage until seven."

"Okay, I'm working dinner again tonight, since I'm off weekends for a while. Ride carefully, and I'll see you later."

"Will do."

He backed out of the house before she decided to quiz him about the tutoring job. He hadn't meant for her to see the clothes, but now hiding them seemed both stupid and shortsighted. She saw the laundry when she took it to the Laundromat. Of course she'd see the new clothes.

The whole ride to school, he worried. Mom was too thin, and she looked so tired. He wished Dad wasn't such a deadbeat—he was a trust-fund baby for God's sake. And he wished even more that Mom didn't have to work so hard to keep them fed. As soon as he graduated college and had a real job, Ben was going to send even more money home to her. Part three of the Ben Franklin future plan.

He arrived at school about twenty minutes before bell. As soon as he saw his reflection in somebody's car window, he groaned. Yep, the helmet had crunched everything, and he was back to looking like a hedgehog.

"Ben!"

Salvation! Paige was trotting in his direction, her eyes wide with amusement. "I know, I know," he said. "I can't help it—riding my bike made a mess."

"Did you bring your gel?" she asked. When he nodded, she gave his sleeve a tug. "Let's go to my car to fix it before you go inside."

He let himself be dragged over to her Mustang. Once settled, he handed her the tube and closed his eyes as she worked her fingers across his scalp and through his hair. Goose bumps rose first on his neck, then on his arms, and he worried he might be drooling because, man, she was a pro. "Mmmm."

"Um, I don't speak caveman," she said.

Now she was tugging gently on small sections of his hair, and he was suddenly aware that this was a lot more intimate than any kiss. What was she doing to him? What were *they* doing? God, he hoped she'd never stop. He blew out a long, slow breath to calm down and mumbled, "Could...learn."

She laughed softly and leaned closer. His eyes snapped open as her chest pressed against his arm. The scent of her perfume was everywhere. *She* was everywhere. His entire field of vision was made up of warm brown eyes, creamy skin, and freckles. He hadn't noticed the freckles on the bridge of her nose, but he liked the quirk. It kept her from being too perfect. And why hadn't he noticed the way her T-shirts stretched tight across her chest, or the fact that her legs were lean and tan and her skirt was so short—

"What were you saying?" she whispered.

With effort, he focused on her face again. Was she allowed to wear a skirt that short to school? "Uh, what?"

Her smile was vaguely coy. "I didn't hear what you said when I was fixing your hair."

"Oh, um, I said you should learn. To speak caveman."

He swallowed hard, and his hands were shaking. He had this irresistible urge to wrap his arms around her, maybe tangle his fingers in *her* hair, while kissing... *Stop it. Just. Stop.* "And you should look into a career as a high-dollar massage therapist, because oh my God."

Paige sat up straight, smiling. "Look at your hair."

He sat up, too, then pulled down the visor to check himself in the vanity mirror. "Whoa! This looks better than when Joey did it."

"Joey likes a more punk-rock look than most girls do." She pointed at his head. "This screams, 'I'm a little bit good and a little bit bad. Take your pick.' Pay close attention to the girls you pass in the hall today. I expect a report back on the reactions."

The way she said it sounded like she was proud of her work but also not sure she wanted girls looking at him. And why did she always seem so sad? There were dark circles under her eyes he hadn't noticed when she was massaging his scalp—hell, he hadn't noticed a *lot* of things when she was doing that. Paige seemed to be hanging on by a thread, and worry crept through him. He wanted to help, but he had no idea what to do other than stick to the program.

"Okay," he whispered. "Whatever you want."

She flashed him a weak smile, then climbed out of the Mustang. They walked slowly toward the school. "I don't know how to thank you for all this," he said.

"Yes, you do," she said when they reached the front doors. "Now, go get 'em, tiger."

Chapter Seventeen

Paige

Paige hurried down the hall, trying to put some distance between herself and Ben. God, she'd been two seconds away from jumping him in her car. It had sounded so simple when she offered to help fix his hair, but sitting close together, with his head bent toward hers…it had tugged at every nerve. He smelled like Ivory soap mixed with a hint of sweat from his ride. That should've bothered her, but it didn't. No, she'd taken *way* too much time with his hair just so she could breathe him in like she was addicted.

He'd been checking her out, too. She'd seen how he looked at her legs, how he had trouble staying focused on her face. Was it possible? Could he start to like her instead of Zoey? The way he reacted to her scalp massage—ha, never saw that coming, did he?—was sexy as hell. He'd practically started moaning, and she was dying to find out what *else* she could do to elicit that kind of reaction from him.

Zoey was at her locker when Paige walked up, and she cocked her head, examining her for a long moment. "You're flushed. Are you coming down with something?"

A bad case of Ben-itis, most likely. "Don't think so."

"I just wondered because you've been acting a little off the last few days." Zoey leaned against her locker door and swung her blond hair over one shoulder. "Please tell me what's bothering— Dang…who's the new guy?"

Paige turned and nearly choked on her own oxygen. Ben was taking a casual stroll down their end of senior hall. His first class was on the other side of the building, so this was definitely suspicious. Had he taken her offhand comment to gauge other girls' reactions too seriously?

"Um…he's not new," Paige said. "His name is Ben. He's in my AP English class."

"Ben…Ben…" Zoey's bright blue eyes flew open wide. "Oh, wow…he looks a little like the guy from the tire store. The sweet one who tried to work my car in early the other day."

"That…sounds like something he would do," Paige murmured.

He walked past them, nodding like he was a cowboy tipping his hat, and Zoey giggled. Paige rolled her eyes at him, then buried her head in her locker.

"He's funny," Zoey said. "Wonder why I've never noticed him?"

Paige gritted her teeth. *Because you never notice guys around here? Because you have a thing for college guys who look like Chris Pine? Because you don't realize how many hearts you break on this campus?*

But all she said was, "He's had a few honors classes with me. He's quiet. Keeps to himself mostly."

"You know him?"

Oh, no. Zoey was showing an interest. An actual interest. The last time she'd even noticed a guy at Alderwood was sophomore year with Jace. Then she'd gone off to Aspen with her parents and when she came back, she didn't talk to him again. Noticing Ben was good…and bad.

So very, very bad.

No, the angel on her shoulder said, *it's good, Paige. Ben wants Zoey to notice him, and it's working. If you care anything about him, take the high road.*

The devil on her other shoulder was shouting, *Fuck the high road!* but, alas, Perfect Paige would never do that.

"Yes. He's nice," she forced herself to say. "Want me to introduce you?"

"Oh, I was just curious." Zoey flashed her a distracted smile and swung her purse onto her shoulder. "See you at lunch, right?"

"Sure."

As Zoey walked away, Paige sighed as boys' heads turned from every direction to watch the sway of her hips. How could she ever hope to compete with that? If she introduced Ben to Zoey, she'd lose any chance with him she might've had.

But it meant *so much* to him…and she didn't break promises.

No matter what that darn devil was shouting.

She slammed her locker door shut and trudged to English, worried about seeing Ben. When she arrived at the classroom, though, he had his nose buried in the book they were reading—*The Metamorphosis* by Kafka. Why Mrs. Cinster thought reading about a guy turning into a giant roach was a good idea, Paige didn't know, but now the sight gave her a pang. Ben was going through his own, more positive, change. And it wasn't going unnoticed.

Two girls who sat up front with Paige were giggling behind their hands, taking quick looks at him. From the sound of the giggles, they weren't making fun. Oh, no, these were *appreciative* giggles. She slumped in her seat as the bell rang. At least she had concrete proof she did good work. Just call her the Professor Higgins of Alderwood High. Would Ben consent to being called Eliza Doolittle? Doubtful.

"Paige, can you talk about how Grete's affections for her brother Gregor change over the course of the novella?" Mrs. Cinster asked out of nowhere.

This was what she deserved for watching AMC on Saturday mornings and letting her mind wander in class. But she knew the material, and she knew how Grete felt. "At first she took good care of him, but as time went on, and her own life outside the house expanded and improved, she started to see him as a duty. A nuisance. Almost like Kafka is saying that growing up makes people jerks."

A laugh rippled through the room, but Mrs. Cinster was nodding. "And? What do you think about that?"

Thinking about Ben and Zoey, Daddy and med school, Stanford and calculus, she answered, "I think figuring out your place in life is hard. I also think Gregor was poorly treated. All he ever wanted was to help his family—even if he did resent it a little—and have them love him in return. But they didn't. Because he wasn't good enough for them after he turned into a bug. They liked the pretty sister better."

Mrs. Cinster was almost clapping her hands in delight, and she went on to ask someone else to talk about Gregor's parents, leaving Paige to sink deeper into her desk. She felt Ben's stare and knew he was watching her, maybe worried, maybe not. It didn't matter. She was the bug. She'd always be the bug. And the idea made her want to scream.

Chapter Eighteen

BEN

Ben watched Paige for most of English, wishing he could whisper in her ear, tell her she'd be okay. She was huddled in on herself, almost like she was cold, but he knew better. She'd been so sad the night before. What had her parents said about him after she went home? That had to be what the whole "he wasn't good enough for them as a bug" comment was about. The problem was, he couldn't decide if she was talking about the way her parents saw him...or how she thought they saw *her*.

A sense of resolve settled over him. Whether the Westfields didn't approve of him or if they just wanted their daughter to focus entirely on school didn't matter. He wouldn't make trouble for Paige. No more sitting in her car with her fingers in his hair. They'd study in the library, and he'd keep his hands—and daydreams—to himself.

Besides, Zoey had smiled at him this morning. He'd strutted down that hallway, pretending to be confident on Paige's order, and he'd loved the attention. But Zoey's smile didn't affect him as much as seeing her at the tire store had, and that had only been a few days ago. No—he'd been more interested in Paige's reaction. Her wide-eyed stare had made him feel like a rock star. And when she'd rolled her eyes… it had been all he could do not to start cracking up. She just made everything easier, even acting like a pretty-boy d-bag swaggering down senior hall.

More reason to stay away from her. Maybe if he knew Zoey better, she'd start to like him, and he'd like her, and everything would work out like he planned. So, when the bell rang, he didn't wait for Paige. Some distance would be good for both of them.

The day went by fast, and he had to admit his new look was getting plenty of attention. Why hadn't he noticed how many girls went to this school? Everywhere he went, stares and whispers followed. He'd have to report back to Paige. Then he remembered he wouldn't see her after school to-day—tomorrow, either. They weren't due to study until Saturday morning, and he had to keep those boundaries set.

His breath hitched painfully. The thought of staying away from Paige hurt, which only made all of this harder.

After fifth period, he headed to his locker. Kent expected him at the garage as fast as he could pedal today. As he was leaving, a girl called out, "Ben? It's Ben, right?"

He turned and there was Zoey, shining in all her glory. She flipped her blond hair over her shoulder, and his brain took a sharp left turn. Huh, had anyone ever accidentally run off the highway after catching sight of her? Because that was totally plausible in his opinion.

Somehow, he managed a smile. "Yes."

"Nice to meet you for real." She flashed him a brilliant smile in return. "Paige pointed you out today, and I realized you were the boy from the tire store. I'm sorry I was kind of a brat about having to wait. I was just running late…you ever have one of those days when everything goes wrong?"

"All the time," he said, still grinning like a jerk. God, he needed to pull it together.

"Thank you for trying to help me, though." She touched his arm, and his eyes widened. Zoey Miller *touched* his arm! "Look, I'm having a party weekend after next, for Halloween. I'm asking Paige to come, too. Want to join us?"

"Um, yeah, sure. That sounds great."

"Perfect!" She released his arm, still smiling. "See you then."

He stood there, paralyzed, as she walked away. Zoey Miller had just asked him to a party. How the hell did that happen? Was Paige right—did she really have the 411 on what her best friend liked in a guy?

He dashed outside and raced for his bike, already late for work, but it was worth it. The whole ride was a blur of trees and the burbling creek singing of his triumph. All he could see was Zoey, smiling at him. That's when the nerves set in. He'd never been to an A-lister party. What should he wear? How should he act? Did he need to bring anything? Paige could help; he'd just have to ask.

He skidded to a halt behind the tire store, because it hit him…if he was going to show up at Zoey's house, he *had* to have Paige's help. He couldn't arrive on his bike, and he needed to walk in with someone who knew what was going on, otherwise he'd never make it through the front door. He'd be too chicken to go inside without her.

Would Paige be okay with that? She didn't know how he felt about her, at least he didn't think so, but he didn't want to put her in the awkward spot of babysitting him, either. He'd wait to talk to her about it Saturday. This might be something to talk over in person. He parked his bike, mulling it over, and went inside to change.

When he made it into the garage, Juan let out a long wolf whistle. "Franklin, you're stylin' today."

The other guys chuckled, and Kent came around the corner. He took one look and shook his head. "What, were there boy-band auditions at school?"

"Ha ha," he said. "Can't a guy get a haircut without all of you being psycho about it?"

"Sure, but not if you're going to come in here looking like a Hemsworth," Kent said. "On the other hand, we have a lot of ladies in the waiting room. Maybe you should work the desk today, slick."

Ben picked up the air wrench. "No, thanks. I'm good slinging tires."

Everyone left him alone after that, although Juan came by to ruffle his hair, exclaiming, "Ow! I cut my hand on that gel, man!"

He was definitely going to need a hat for work from now on.

Chapter Nineteen

Paige filled the time until her next study session by trying to cram in as much homework as her brain would allow. It was a good way to keep her mind off Ben, but it was still hard. He smiled when he saw her in English Friday morning, which was almost enough to crack her determination not to complicate her life.

But then she caught him flashing that same smile at Zoey in the hall, and she found it a little easier to ignore him. Mixed signals, thy name was Ben Effing Franklin.

Making matters worse, Zoey had decided, out of nowhere, to have a Halloween party in a week. She and Alana were deep in conversation about it when Paige hit her locker Friday afternoon.

"So what should I go as?" Alana asked, forehead wrinkled. Today's outfit included green capris printed with pink flamingos and a matching pink polo. Just how many Lilly Pulitzer outfits did she have? "I'm thinking an angel."

Zoey snorted. "Girl, you're no angel. If anyone should be the angel, it's sweetie here." She gave Paige a side-hug. "She's nice to everyone and never gets into trouble."

The devil on Paige's shoulder—the one who had been bugging her the last few days—put a hand on her hip and blew a raspberry. "What party?"

"We're having a Halloween party at Zoey's," Alana said. "Costumes, candy—the whole tamale."

"Enchilada. The whole enchilada," Paige murmured.

"Oh, whatever." She waved an airy hand. "Want to help us plan it?"

The automatic "yes" was on the tip of her tongue, but exhaustion made her think twice. She had so much on her plate—maybe it was time to stop saying yes to everything. "I wish I could. I have a lot going on right now."

Alana looked put out, but Zoey nudged her. "Totally understand. You'll still come, right?"

"Of course."

One of the football players called out to Alana, and she scurried away as fast as her pink flip-flops would take her. Once she was gone, Zoey looked Paige over. "You going to tell me?"

She busied herself with opening her locker. "I don't know what you mean."

"What's bothering you." Zoey's eyes were full of concern. "Girl...talk to me."

The thing was—she *couldn't*. Even if she wanted to, even if the worried expression on Zoey's face made her want to break down crying, she couldn't tell. "Lots of pressure from the parents, uh, about college stuff. And the piano recital."

"Right, I forgot the recital." She patted Paige's arm. "You're going to do great. Try not to stress so much, okay? And don't feel bad about turning us down to help with the party. I know you're crazy busy, even if no one else seems to get it."

Paige managed a weak smile. "Thanks."

Funny enough—she did feel a little better. Zoey was a good friend. Maybe it wouldn't suck completely if she and Ben started going out.

Friday afternoon, after a stop at the ElderCare center to drop off the check from the bake sale, along with the number of a reputable used piano dealer her mom knew, she went home to study. It was a beautiful day, warm, with a soft southern breeze. Why study in the house when she could escape outside to read the chapters for psychology? Only seniors were allowed to take it, and she loved the subject so far. They were studying life stages and Erickson's theory of psychosocial development. It was interesting—and hit way too close to home—to read his theory that the main psychological crisis for adolescents was "identity versus role confusion" and development of a unified sense of self.

And if that wasn't a "no shit, Sherlock" statement, she didn't know a better one.

"Sweet Pea? What are you doing out here?" Daddy called from the back door.

"Studying," she said. "Psychology, to be exact. You know what I'm thinking?"

"No, what are you thinking?" He came out and sat next to her. He had a lite beer in hand and had already changed into shorts and a linen shirt. Dark stubble lined his jaw, and his eyelids drooped. He always looked spent by the time Friday rolled around. Being a doctor was hard—Daddy never had any real time off.

"Well, Erickson talks about how the elderly are concerned—psychologically at least—with having a sense of a life well lived. But that's not true for your patients, is it? They're stuck on the identity crisis."

"Regressed back to that phase, more like, but yes." His eyes lit up. "You're onto something. Keep thinking through it like that, and you'll make a great neurologist."

She forced herself to nod. Would she ever be as good a doctor as he was? "I was wondering something else. What made you want to be a doctor?"

"The science," he said right away. "I like looking at puzzles—my patients—and trying to find the right solution. That's why I went into clinical research. Alzheimer's is a problem screaming for a solution as our population ages. Running trials is the best chance we have of finding something that works."

"But what about the people side?" She loved her buddies at the ElderCare center. The science seemed less important when you were trying to help an eighty-year-old woman remember her son from the pictures in her room. "They're *human* puzzles."

"A good bedside manner is always important. You build relationships—sometimes more with the families than the patients once they're in the advanced stages—but it's the science that matters most. Diagnosis, treatment, observation." He squeezed her shoulder, his eyes shining. "And you, Sweet Pea, are going to make an outstanding scientist. You have an analytical mind, just like your old dad. We'll find a cure one day. We'll stand side-by-side in the lab and we'll see something work for the first time. Won't that be something?"

Paige's heart sank. All this time, she'd gone along with this plan, thinking she'd be taking care of people, helping. And she would be, but not in the way she'd hoped. Now that she knew what Daddy's job was like, research, running tests on patient after patient to find a cure...was that what she wanted? She would be healing people. It just wouldn't be the same as sitting at their bedsides, making those connections she loved so much.

"How was work?" she asked timidly. "You look tired."

"I lost a patient today." He took a long swig of beer, staring out at the pool. "Not one you know from the center, but a grandmother of seven. Her family was devastated. That's why we need to figure out Alzheimer's, Pea. It takes away the best in people...it's cruel. And it'll take good scientists to unlock the answer."

"I'm sorry," she murmured. "Well, I'd better finish reading before Mom calls us to dinner."

"Is that a nice way of telling me to be quiet?"

She smiled. "Possibly."

He held up his beer in a silent toast, and they sat together quietly. Paige found she couldn't read, though, so she faked it, turning pages every so often to make it look good. All the while, her brain was racing through her life and, more than ever, she had no idea who the real Paige Westfield was—or who she wanted to be. If being a doctor, a clinical researcher like Daddy, meant being a scientist first and a healer second...could she be happy doing that for a living? She couldn't think of people as science projects—they had names, families.

The sun was on its way down when Mom called them to dinner. Daddy went to hold the door for Paige, but her phone buzzed. "Go ahead. I'll just be a minute."

He nodded and went inside. The smell of poached salmon wafted out as the door closed. Gag. Just for once, couldn't her mother make lasagna or tacos for dinner? Sighing, she picked up her phone.

Ben: *Hey! What time are we meeting tomorrow? I have to be at my other job at one.*

P: *How's ten?*

B: *Where?*

She stared out over their backyard, seeing it through his eyes. The landscaping, the stone-patterned patio floor, the gleaming pool. She really wanted him to come here, to see if she could break the ice with her parents some, but she'd have to have a long talk with them at dinner first. And how about Ben? Would he even want to study here?

She'd have to dangle a real carrot to make that happen. Something to continue their plan to win over Zoey. Wait… there was one thing, a plan that would definitely get Zoey's attention—and have a little added bonus for her, too.

P: *My place. Want me to pick you up?*

There was a very long pause. Mom called through the screen door, "Dinner's getting cold."

"In a minute!"

She could hear her parents mumbling about, "Angsty

angst," before Mom closed the interior door. Yeah, they'd see some angsty angst if they didn't behave tomorrow.

Assuming Ben said yes.

Another two minutes ticked by, and she wondered if he was going to answer at all, when her phone buzzed again.

B: *Will your parents mind?*

P: *Not sure I care. I had an idea about Zoey, but you'll need to be here for it to work.*

She waited through another two-minute pause—he was really having to think this over. Ugh, had Mom scared him away for good?

Finally, he replied: *Okay. I remember your address, so I don't need a ride. See you at ten.*

Triumphant, she marched into the kitchen and announced, "Ben's coming over tomorrow to study. Any objections?"

Her parents exchanged a glance, then Mom said, "The boy from the other night?"

As if she didn't remember. Puh-lease. "Yes, Mom. Look, I know you and Daddy would feel better if I only studied with the stuck-up jackasses at the country club, but Ben is super smart and a good study partner. I want to nail my transcripts this semester, so try to be nice."

They exchanged an even more freaked out look. She guessed the cursing was a bit shocking. Maybe her little shoulder-devil was taking over more than she thought.

Maybe that wasn't a terrible thing.

Dad held up a hand. "Sweet Pea, I'm sure he's a fine young man—"

"That's sounds too much like you're saying 'no,'" she said sharply. "He's a very nice guy. If you just got over his address, you'd see that. He's coming over, and I promise he won't steal the silver."

Mouths hung open across the table, and her feeling of triumph surged. She might not know who she wanted to be, but right now, she knew exactly what she wanted, and her parents needed to know it.

"As long as you stay downstairs, it's fine for him to come here and study with you," Mom said, sounding resigned. "We just want what's best for you, honey."

"No, you want what you *think* is best for me." She shoved her chair back. The smell of salmon was making her sick, and she'd lost her appetite. She walked to the back staircase but paused before going up. "Oh, Ben and I are going to wash my car while he's here."

Chapter Twenty

BEN

When Ben finally made it home from the tire store, Mom was already there. A heavenly smell hit him as he came in through the side door.

"Is that fried chicken?" he asked, sniffing the whole way to the kitchen. "Please tell me it is."

She turned from the stove, looking pleased. "It's rare I'm off on a Friday evening, so I thought we'd live it up a little. Besides, a whole fryer was on sale."

He tried not to feel guilty about wanting the chicken, but he couldn't help it. "I'm sorry, Ma."

"Whatever for?" She deftly turned over pieces of chicken in the skillet. The cooked sides were a perfect golden color, and his mouth watered.

"About…" What *was* he sorry about? Their paycheck-to-paycheck life? Watching her work so damned hard for so little? Him, having to work so hard for the things that came so easily to other students at Alderwood?

"Is this about a girl?" Mom asked. The chicken popped and crackled as it fried. "Because you look like a kid who has girl trouble."

"What? No!"

She sniffed. "Uh-huh. The haircut…the new outfits." When he opened his mouth to make an excuse, she held up a hand. "I have no problem with that part. I'm just wondering who the lucky girl is, to have a boy try so hard to impress her?"

That was the question, wasn't it? He wanted to say Zoey, because it was easier. But Paige was on his mind every other minute. Maybe tomorrow, after being on the receiving end of Mrs. Westfield's death-ray stares, it would be easier to focus on Zoey. For now, though…

"And he said it wasn't a girl," Mom purred, smirking. "Okay, bud, who is she? Answer or no chicken."

"Dang, Ma, you're mean."

"Eh, I just fight dirty." She pulled a crispy, golden chicken leg out of the skillet and laid it on a paper-towel-lined plate. "Mmmm. Smells good, doesn't it?"

His stomach rumbled, and her smirk widened. If there was ever a time to pull his hair out, this was it. "Fine. There's a girl. She's nice, pretty, and…" Paige's face floated into his mind. "Smart. Driven. She's thinking of becoming a doctor."

"Sounds like the kind of girl I'd want you to date." Mom put the chicken leg onto a fresh plate and handed it to him. "Tell me more."

"It's complicated."

"Oh, good. I was worried it'd be too easy." When he shot

her a frustrated look, her expression softened into a kind smile. "Love that's too easy isn't worth much. It's better when there's some work involved."

"What about you and Dad? You seemed to work hard." Or fight. Whichever.

"No, we had it way too easy in the beginning. He was handsome, and I was fun, and we had a very intense, marvelous time. Which is why when things were tough, he bolted. You want a girl who drives you crazy but would wade through wet cement to get to you."

That sounded a little—or a lot—like Paige. She was definitely willing to take the hard way on things. And she definitely drove him crazy.

"It's just...I kind of like this other girl, too. She's *also* gorgeous and popular and nice. I'm having trouble figuring out what to do."

Mom calmly wiped her hands on a dishtowel, then walked over to the table and gave him a little smack on the back of the head. "Don't be that guy. I raised you better."

"Hey! What, can't I like two people?"

"Yes, but you can only date one at a time." Mom's voice was stern. "That was a preemptive scolding. Don't two-time. Got it? Decide which girl you want to go out with and stick with her until you know it's working or not. I like the sound of the doctor girl, myself. Just saying."

He laughed. "You don't even know either of them."

"Mother's intuition. Besides, you spent more time describing her than the other girl. You should think on that."

His ears flamed up, and the flush spread down the back of his neck. Mom was right, but would Paige even consider going out with him? She was so stone-cold focused on

Stanford he wasn't sure she even wanted to go out with any-one, let alone someone her parents might not approve of. He'd have to pay attention tomorrow and see what his gut told him. Unlike his mom, his intuition about girls was crap.

"I will. Promise." He held up his chicken leg. "Can I eat now?"

She laughed. "Dig in."

The next morning, he skimmed the week's math lessons so he'd be ready to help Paige, then went out to his bike. The air was humid, and he swore he could taste the scent of heated tar coming from the pothole filler lining his street. Paige's neighborhood probably smelled like flowers, grass, and chlorine from all the pools.

Traffic was light along the main drag near the tire store, and he made it to the greenbelt quicker than usual, which allowed him to slow his pace and enjoy the sound of the wind in the trees. His calc book bounced against his back in his bag, padded by his movie theater uniform. He had the afternoon and evening shift, which he liked. He finished his shift at ten, instead of two a.m., and he was off tomorrow for a change. He'd tried to sign up for an extra shift, but the theater was fully staffed, and Kent's store was closed on Sundays. As much as he needed the cash, he was kind of relieved. He could use the time to catch up on his physics homework without staying up past midnight.

The greenbelt gave way to the hills surrounding the country club. As he pulled into Paige's neighborhood, the sounds switched to lawnmowers and leaf blowers. Land-scaping crews were out in force, taking care of all those per-fect, huge yards. The lawn guys looked up as he pedaled past, giving him quick nods. They knew he didn't belong here, that they had some things in common. Who did they think he was—a babysitter? A boy toy? That made him laugh, but anything was possible.

There was a long hill leading up to Paige's cul-de-sac he hadn't noticed while riding in her car the other night, but he noticed it now. He was puffing and his thighs were burning by the time he reached her driveway.

Mrs. Westfield was out front, pruning her roses in a sunhat and matching gardening gloves. She looked kind of ridiculous, but it was her garden. She could look ridiculous if she wanted to. Honestly, he was surprised to see her out here, getting her hands dirty, instead of standing on the porch, telling the lawn crew what to do.

She glanced up when he stepped off his bike. Her expression fought between distrust and politeness. "Hello, Ben."

"H-hello," he panted, before sucking down a deep breath, too tired to be intimidated. His shirt was stuck to his back and his hair was damp with sweat. Not the impression he wanted to make. "Is Paige home?"

She stared at him a long moment, then sighed. "She's out back."

Mrs. Westfield turned back to her roses, not giving him any hint as to where "out back" was or how to find it. Shrugging, he parked his bike at the side of the driveway and went around the house, looking for a backyard gate. Through the fence, he could hear Paige on the phone.

"Yeah, the purple one... Is that okay?... Thanks. See you in a bit."

Ben spotted an ornate cedar and wrought-iron gate and let himself into the yard. Paige was sitting at a patio table with her books spread out around her. For a minute, he stood next to the house and watched her. Her dark curls fluttered in the breeze, and a little line creased her forehead while she worked. He wanted to kiss the worry away—but that kind of thinking would get them both into trouble with her parents nearby.

If she didn't smack him on the nose first.

And he shouldn't be standing here, watching her. He cleared his throat and walked over to the table. She smiled when he joined her, but things felt off between them. Before Thursday, there'd been some spark, some life, but now she guarded every emotion.

"Was my mom rude?" she asked.

"She was...preoccupied. With her flowers."

She snorted. "Sorry. I don't know why her panties are in a knot. Anyway, I was thinking we could study out here. It's nice with the fan on."

He glanced up. Their patio was fully decked out with a wood-beam ceiling and fans whirring overhead. "Definitely." He took a seat across from her, thinking she'd welcome distance, even if it would be harder to work on her calculus this way. "Where should we start?"

"I'm having trouble with Limits," she said.

Her cheeks flushed after she said that, which gave him some hope. "Are we still talking about calculus? Or something more interesting?"

Paige held herself very still and was quiet long enough he wondered if he'd be asked to leave soon. Finally, she nodded slowly. "Just calculus."

Okay, whatever was going on with her was off-limits... yeah, nice math pun there, dork. Not asking what was wrong took some effort, but he pulled out his book. "Then let's get started."

"Good. Because I have a little activity planned after this."

Her voice was light, and his pulse leaped up ten beats a minute. An activity, like her massaging his scalp again? Did she think he was interested in that kind of activity? Because he definitely was. "Oh?"

"Yep. Phase two in the 'get a date with Zoey' plan."

His heart slowed like he'd hit a wall. He'd forgotten to tell her he'd been invited to Zoey's party. "Look, there's—"

"Nope, no questions until after we study." She brandished a mechanical pencil in his direction—it was pink. "So, Limits."

He held in a sigh. He'd tell her about the party later. "All right. Limits."

It took almost two hours to finish her homework. She was trying, but unlike Wednesday, she seemed to be struggling more. No matter how he tried to explain it to her, it wouldn't sink in. At one point, she literally pulled at her own hair and kicked the table leg.

"I'm so freaking stupid!" she snapped. "Why can't I do this right?"

"Hey, you aren't stupid. You're too hard on yourself. Am I not explaining things well?" he asked, frustrated he couldn't seem to teach her today. "Or is this concept confusing for you?"

She slammed her book shut. "Sorry. I'm just having a tough day. I hope I haven't wasted your time."

Her tone was stiff, almost hurt, and he felt like crap for setting her off more. "You haven't. I'm worried I'm not helping you like a professional tutor would."

"It's not you." She turned away, but not before he saw tears brimming in her eyes.

Before he knew what he was going to do, he'd pushed back his chair and gone around to kneel in front of her. Laying his hand on hers, he asked, "Want to tell me?"

She squeezed her eyes shut, and her face seemed to crumple as she started to shake with sobs. Whoa, he had no idea how to handle this. Panicking a little, he pulled her to her feet, then sat in her chair and settled her on his lap. She leaned against him, her body a warm weight that seemed to set things right, at least for him, and her perfume lingered on the air, already familiar. Even when Paige turned her head to cry on his shoulder, something inside him relaxed. This, holding her, felt too right to be wrong.

"Please tell me I didn't do something to upset you," he whispered. "Because that would suck."

She cried harder. God, he was so lame, and terrible at comforting crying girls. He clamped his mouth shut to keep from blurting out anything else stupid and rocked her back and forth.

"It's my dad," she eventually murmured into his neck.

He tried to ignore the goose bumps rising on his arms when he felt her breath on his skin. "What about your dad? Did he hurt you?"

"No, not like that." She pulled away and stood.

He instantly missed her warmth and the way she'd felt, pressed against him. *Focus, Ben. Crying girl, here.* "What happened?"

"I was studying psychology last night, and I just had this...epiphany. That being a clinical research doctor might not be the path I should take. I love being with people, talking to them, taking care of them. But when my dad came outside, he was saying what a great scientist I'd be, and how proud he was, and I felt so guilty for doubting myself."

"I can see how that would be tough. But, Paige, if you're not sure you want to go into clinical research, you shouldn't put so much pressure on yourself about Stanford. You can go to med school here and be the kind of doctor who spends time with her patients."

"You don't understand. This has been 'the plan' since forever. My parents are depending on me to take over Daddy's practice." She teared up again, making her voice thick. "Mom…Mom expects me to be the best."

"Then that's their problem," he said, with real force.

She sniffled, and her cheeks were blotchy from the tears. "Yeah…you know what she said to me at the start of the year? That she knew I'd try my hardest to be top of our class because she believed I could be the valedictorian. It's like… it's like being fourth isn't enough."

"And they're pressuring you into medical school on top of it," he said. What would it be like if Mom pushed him like that? She never would—she had stuck his acceptance letter to A&M on the fridge and smiled every time she saw it. Was this why Paige had so much trouble with calc? Was she so afraid to fail and disappoint her parents that she'd paralyzed herself with fear? "That's messed up, okay? Maybe they don't see it that way, but it's really not all that fair to you."

She wiped her eyes with her fingertips. "Maybe. But maybe it's for the best, since I have no idea what I really want to do."

He stood and put his hands on her shoulders. "You

should follow your heart."

"Is that what you're doing?"

He froze. Did she know? Did she see how his feelings had changed about her? About Zoey? "Um, what?"

She blushed and slid into her chair, as if she had just realized she'd been crying in front of him—while sitting on his lap. "Being an engineer. Are you doing that because you're following your heart? Or is it because you think that's what's expected."

The knot in his stomach loosened. She hadn't guessed, then. "I've wanted to be an engineer ever since I was ten and took apart our old microwave, then put it back together. Mom was furious, but when it worked even better than before, she started checking out engineering books from the library for me."

"I'm envious. That you've known what you want to be all this time." She patted his arm, all business now, even though he could tell she was putting on a brave act. "But enough about all this. You don't want to spend what's left of your time off listening to me whine. Are you ready for phase two?"

Was he? Truthfully, he would've listened to her talk about her future all day...but she was finally smiling, so whatever phase two was, she was looking forward to it. "Please tell me you aren't going to put highlights in my hair or pierce my ear."

"No," she said, laughing. "You'd look weird with an earring. Doesn't suit you. No, we're conducting a little experiment today. Come with me." She led him around the four-car garage to where her Mustang was parked in the driveway. "Wait here."

Her mom had gone inside, so Ben took a minute to

stretch and shake the intensity of their conversation loose. Did Paige have anyone to talk to, other than him? How was she holding up under the pressure if there wasn't someone to help her carry the weight? He hurt for her, but a little, selfish part of him was glad he'd been there to hold her while she cried. Even better, she was acting less stiff around him and more like the fierce, determined Paige he'd come to like so much.

She came out of the garage a moment later, carrying a hose, a bucket filled with sponges, and a bottle of Simple Green cleaning solution.

"Washing your car is conducting an experiment?" Ben asked, squinting in the harsh mid-October sunlight. North Texas had three seasons: hot, cold, and rainy. Today was most definitely hot, especially after sitting in the shade under those ceiling fans. After spending all week in the sweltering garage at the tire store, working in the noonday sun didn't sound like his idea of a good time. What was she up to?

"Yes." She tossed him a sponge, then started spraying water into a plastic bucket. Foamy suds rose above the edge. "Trust me."

Trust her, she said. He did, but right now it seemed like she was pranking him. Was she pissed he'd seen her cry? Then again, how did this apply to "phase two" of the Zoey plan?

"Hey, get over here," Paige called, pointing at his sponge. "We're on a timetable."

Curious and more than a little concerned, he plunged the sponge into the soapy water, then went to work washing the Mustang's side panels. Just what was this going to accomplish?

Sixty seconds later, he found out.

Chapter Twenty-One

PAIGE

Was she doing the right thing? Was giving Ben up to Zoey worth the hurt? Because, God, the way he'd held her while she cried had just about broken whatever self-control she had left. If she'd been able to stop crying, she probably would've kissed him right then, to hell with nosy parents. But she knew—she *knew*—if Zoey saw who he really was, he'd be out of her life and into Zoey's. He was just too special. Her best friend would see it right away, and she'd never let him go.

"So why are we doing this again?" he called.

Even though he had no idea what she had in mind for this little stage play, he'd gone along with good humor. Hell, he was even washing her car for real. Which funny because a clean car was beside the point in this plan.

"Just keep doing what you're doing and all will become

crystal clear."

He gave her a long, weird look, then shrugged and went back to work. Paige joined him but spent part of her time focused on the street corner. Any minute now…

"Your tires are low," Ben said, peeking at her around the front bumper. "If you have an air compressor, I could air them up for you."

She propped her fist on her hip. "Does this look like the kind of house that keeps an air compressor on hand?"

He made a face, then laughed. "No, this looks like the kind of house where they call the dealership for help."

"Exactly."

They worked in silence until—there! Paige snapped to get his attention just as Zoey turned onto her street. Ben looked at her, and from the startled expression, she knew she was going to have to coach him through every second of this close encounter.

She gave him a stern look. "Take off your shirt."

His already flushed face turned a deeper shade of red. "What? No way!"

Zoey had pulled up to the curb, and the BMW idled while she dipped out of view, probably to grab her purse. They only had a few seconds, and desperate times called for desperate measures. Paige stalked over to the hose and, under the guise of washing the suds off her car, "accidentally" sprayed Ben right in the chest.

His eyes popped wide open as he stared down at his soaked shirt. "Why?" he growled under his breath.

"Off," Paige growled back, then turned to greet Zoey. "Hey! Thanks for letting me borrow your dress for the party next weekend."

Zoey handed her a dress bag, looking at something beyond Paige's left shoulder. "Yeah, sure."

Zoey didn't say anything else, and Paige hazarded a look behind her. As ordered, Ben had stripped off his shirt and oh…my…God.

Okay, so she had guessed he had nice shoulders under those T-shirts after all the work at the tire store, and she'd definitely copped a feel when they'd cuddled on the back porch, but she couldn't have known he was *that* ripped. He was lean—leaner than most of the football players anyway—but he made the most of what he had, from the tight biceps and defined pecs, right down to the hard, flat stomach and the tantalizing trail of light brown hair running from his navel into the waistband of his shorts…which, oh hell, were riding low on his hips.

She didn't want to blink so she could keep staring. Jesus.

Doing a great job of pretending he didn't notice them hanging on his every move, he reached across the top of the Mustang to soap up the roof. He was a quick study, for sure, stretching in ways that showed off his arms and shoulders. Then he walked over to the bucket and very deliberately bent down to soak the sponge. She might need to sit down. His back was just as good as his front.

She'd created a monster. A very hot, slightly wet monster.

A silent giggle bubbled up from her chest—that had sounded so dirty. Maybe he could wash *her* after the car.

"Um, Paige," Zoey said, giving her a hard nudge. A little smile twitched at the corner of her mouth and her eyes twinkled. "So are you and Ben coming to my party together?"

She couldn't answer. Speech had left the building.

So it was up to Ben, and he played it perfectly. He

flashed Zoey his adorable, bright smile. "I thought we would. I mean, if that's okay? She could give me a ride."

"Great." Zoey scrutinized him a lot longer than Paige felt was necessary. "You know, I was wondering after we talked the other day…did we ever have any classes together? I can't believe we hadn't met before last week."

He stepped away from the car, facing the girls head-on with soap and water dripping down his chest. If her brain hadn't had a misfire, Paige would've been proud of him for carrying on a coherent conversation with Zoey, but she could only stand there, staring, as he said, "Um…yeah. Sophomore year?"

"Homeroom!" Zoey exclaimed, sounding delighted. "Yes! Mrs. Cummings."

He nodded, and they grinned at each other. Paige almost gagged…then imagined puking on Zoey's shoes. That helped a little.

"So." Zoey turned to her. "What are you two up to today?"

Was she asking if Ben was taken? Paige's heart ached, but she forced a cheerful tone. "Homework. Calculus study partners, actually."

"Then why is he washing your car?"

"Uh…" She hadn't thought that far ahead. All she wanted was for Zoey to have a good look at the merchandise, and that had succeeded, for sure. "He, uh—"

"I want to borrow her car because I don't have one of my own," Ben cut in. "She told me I could drive it if I helped wash it. Seemed like a good deal to me."

"Definitely," Zoey purred, her eyes blazing a trail from the top of his head, all the way down to his feet. "It was good seeing you again. Don't forget the party!"

For a second, Paige worried he might blow it by flying into puppy-dog raptures right there in the driveway, but he held it together long enough to say, "We won't."

Zoey went back to her Beemer, pausing to flash her *you're mine, fresh meat* smile at him before driving away.

As soon as her car cleared the corner, Ben started jumping around like an overexcited golden retriever. "That was awesome!" He laughed and laughed. "You should've seen your faces. I should take off my shirt more often."

Yeah, she'd definitely created a monster. But her excitement about the whole thing had faded when she grasped what Zoey meant earlier. She hung the dress bag over the porch railing. "How did you know about the party?"

Ben stopped laughing and had the grace to look uncomfortable. "She asked me on Thursday afternoon as I was leaving school. I was going to ask if you'd go with me." He gave her a pleading look. "I can't go over there without a ride and some lessons on how to act. I've never been to one of your parties before."

Your parties. He still saw her as something separate, different. More reason to let him have his shot at Zoey and move on. But to what? Was she doomed to do what everyone expected her to do? Good old Paige, they'd say. So dependable. Perfect in a crisis, and always *such* a big help. It hurt to be thought of that way. To know her value came from being organized—like no one else had to be, because she'd take care of things.

Well, if she was going to do what was expected, even if it meant protecting Ben from himself, then that's what she should do. Besides, Zoey *was* her best friend…and she could do so much worse, too. Jace Tillman was walking, talking, breathing proof of that.

She turned away to hide how her hands shook on the hose while she sprayed down her car like none of it mattered. "Okay. First rule—don't follow Zoey around at school next week. Show up every once in a while to chat her up, but don't act too interested, because then she'll start to back away." Paige dropped the hose and picked up a towel. "I've seen it. Don't scare her off. Work your way into her life slowly."

"Play it cool. Got it," he said. "What else?"

He looked so excited, and it was just too much. Even he saw her as the "fixer"—and that was after holding her during a meltdown. She'd never let anyone see her crack like that, but she'd hoped he was different...that she could be imperfect around him. The back of her throat ached with the effort of holding back tears. Maybe people couldn't change. Maybe she'd always be the girl who took care of things. And if that was true, then how could she have the slightest bit of hope Ben could care for *her* in Zoey Miller's world?

"Paige?" he asked, sounding so hopeful it cracked her heart. "Anything else I should know?"

Her head ached from the sun glinting off the wet Mustang, and all she wanted was to lie down in a quiet room until it stopped, then take a swim. "Nothing. Leave the rest to me." She dropped the towel and started for the front door. She'd pick everything up later. Her parents wouldn't even notice the mess. "Look, I'm not feeling well. I'm sorry, but I need to go inside."

"Do you need anything?" he asked softly.

Paige kept her back to him, her face scrunched up with the effort not to cry. She wanted to scream at him. Or kiss him. Either would be acceptable, at least to her.

"No," she said. "See you later."

Then she left him standing in the driveway.

Chapter Twenty-Two

BEN

Ben watched her slip inside before throwing the sponge as hard as he could at the garage door, leaving a trail of suds dripping down the side. What the hell just happened? He did exactly what she wanted, then she just left?

He picked up his wet shirt and pulled it over his head. It stuck to his chest and back, but at least he wasn't hot now. He was definitely still bothered, though.

Jesus.

For a while, he'd thought things were going great during the fake car wash. Both Zoey *and* Paige were looking him over like he'd turned into a superhero before their eyes. He'd been shocked by Paige's tactics, but he couldn't argue with the result. He partly hoped Paige had come up with the idea because she wanted him to take off his shirt, using Zoey as a convenient excuse.

Then Zoey had said something about him going to the party with Paige, and his heart had shot right into his throat, thinking he was about to get a chance to see if Paige was into him. That's why he kept asking her about what to do at the party after Zoey left, so she'd say something about going with him, but it backfired and he had no idea why.

Now she was gone, and he was standing in someone else's driveway, all alone. More reason for him to choke off any feelings he had for her. She kept making it really clear she didn't need him beyond their arrangement—he was a complication and she had her own plans for the future. A future where he didn't belong.

But when she cried…

He'd never seen anything like it. She just fell apart. He knew she was having a hard time, but she was struggling even more than he'd guessed. Sure, he had it hard right now, but he knew where he was going and how to get there. She was running as fast as she could toward something she wasn't sure she wanted. All because she couldn't stand disappointing her dad. How was it to live like that? Always worried about messing up, afraid of every step you took?

His brain—and his heart—was tied in knots, neither one of them able to solve the problem of Paige. He might be a math whiz, but she was a puzzle he couldn't put together.

He glanced at the house. Would he ever do things right with her? He didn't know, and that was enough to tell him he needed to be careful with Paige for a while. Besides, trying to figure out what a girl was feeling and thinking was harder than the AP physics exam.

Irritated, he really wanted to hit a brick wall until his hand bled, just to feel better, but instead he finished drying the car, cleaned the sponges, coiled up the hose, then stacked everything neatly beside the garage. If nothing else, she had a clean car now.

He needed to go to work, but his backpack was still on the patio. He'd pick it up, then ride to the theater. A night spent selling popcorn would help him forget this mess. When he let himself into the backyard, though, he ran smack into Dr. Westfield. Like cracked-their-heads-together ran into.

"Ow," Dr. Westfield said, rubbing his temple. "You have one hard head, kid."

He didn't know the half of it. "Sorry, sir. Did I hurt you?"

"Not too badly. I think I'll live." He stuck out a hand. "I'm Paige's dad."

Ben couldn't help but notice the man had manicured nails. What would this doctor think of a working guy's hands? "Nice to meet you."

They shook, then stood there, awkwardly sizing each other up. "So...where's Paige?" Dr. Westfield asked.

"Uh, she said she wasn't feeling well, so she went in. I was just going to grab my bag." He tried to edge around Dr. Westfield, but he blocked the entire path and inched over to keep Ben from making it past.

"Son, I don't know what project the two of you are working on, but she's seemed fairly high-strung the last week. You know anything about that?"

His tone was cold, and his gaze was shrewd. What would he do if he knew Paige was flunking calc? Probably hit the roof. He'd never expect that, though—Perfect Paige didn't fail classes. Obviously the problem had to be the kid from the south side of town. Jackass. "She's under a lot of stress at school. Final transcripts are due."

"I know," Dr. Westfield said. "You going to college?"

He bristled. Did this man think just because he rode a bike and had calluses on his hands he wasn't smart enough to go to college? "I've been accepted to a number of them, so I thought, why not?" he snapped. "But, as you can probably tell, I need a scholarship or seven to afford it, so I'm busting my butt to maintain my place as third in the class."

They stared at each other, then Dr. Westfield's shoulders relaxed. "Paige is number four."

"I know."

"Okay, then." He stepped aside and let Ben through. "It seems you're both committed to doing well on this project. I can accept that."

It was a dismissal, and he'd had enough of those today. "Who gives a crap what you can accept? You don't even know why your daughter is so upset these days, and you have to ask a guy you barely know if he does. If you talked to her instead of telling her how to live her life, she might be a little happier."

Oh, shit.

Dr. Westfield looked like he'd been slapped. Before he could start yelling or asking questions, Ben raced to grab his backpack, then stalked to his bike. God. What had he just done?

How long ago did he decide to be careful with Paige? Five minutes? Ten? And he'd just dared her dad to press her about what was wrong. Idiot.

He pedaled like he was barely staying ahead of the pack at the Hotter'N Hell race, ignoring the sweat running in rivulets down his forehead and back.

Paige was going to kill him. Or worse…never speak to him again.

Chapter Twenty-Three

PAIGE

When Paige woke up, the sun was far to the west. It was too late for a good swim, and besides, she was starving.

What was it about having your soul crushed two days in a row that made you hungry?

She picked up her phone, thinking she'd raid the kitchen, since she doubted anyone was cooking tonight, but stopped short and sank down on her bed.

Zoey had texted—four times:

Z: *My timing was perfect today. Those shoulders. Damn.*

Z: *I went back and looked at the yearbook. Ben's cute. I wonder why I didn't remember him before.*

Z: *Are you* sure *you're just friends?*

Z: *Hello?*

If anything, Paige had proof she was a good matchmaker. What was that movie with J. Lo? *The Wedding Planner—* the one where she fell in love with the groom. He fell in love with her, too, and ditched his wedding for her. Which, if she was honest, didn't really make him the best example of the kind of guy she'd totally respect, but still… Besides, that only happened in movies, and everything was going according to plan here. In just over a week, Ben and Zoey would be a thing, and people would be coming up with cute couple names for them, like Zen.

And Paige would be studying alone.

A lump formed in her throat, but she texted back: *Sorry, nap. Yes, friends. Yeah, he's cute if you like that sort of guy.*

Her phone buzzed immediately.

Z: *What sort of guy? Cute and smart? Because, girl, that's totally your type.*

Anxiety fluttered in Paige's belly. She needed to close off this conversation, and fast.

P: *I don't have a type. I'm too focused on Stanford.*

Z: *It's been eight months since you broke it off with Caleb. You need to live a little. A cute, smart guy would be a good place to start.*

Leave it to Zoey to bring up her ex. Looking back, Caleb

hadn't been the right guy—he was just her first. Well, not her first kiss. That was Braden in fourth grade. But Caleb had been the first—and last—everything else. Funny enough, she hadn't been sad for long after it ended, making her angst over Ben kind of telling. She never hung on Caleb's every word. His compliments never made her blush. He'd been steady, nice. Safe.

Ben was anything but safe. He made her feel too much. As much as she wanted a little uncertainty in her life, she couldn't have it.

P: *Can't really date anyone right now. Too much going on. Maybe in college. How about you? Is Ben your type?*

There, she'd done it.

Except…Zoey didn't answer. The little text bubble didn't even come up. Paige chewed on her lip, waiting. Had Zoey dropped her phone and broken it? Or was something wrong?

Should she text again, or would that look suspicious? Besides, she wasn't sure she could handle a boy-talk session about Ben. She might go all Hulk Smash across the neighborhood. The headlines would light up everywhere: *Crazed teen wrecks golf course community—news at ten.*

Fifteen minutes went by with no answer from Zoey. Giving up, she went downstairs to make a turkey sandwich, praying her mom had accidentally bought real cheese instead of the vegan stuff. Dad was sitting at the kitchen table, a huge salad already in front of him. He smiled when she came in.

"How are you feeling, Sweet Pea? Better?"

She frowned. She hadn't told him she didn't feel well. "Fine. Why do you ask?"

"Oh," he said in a fake cheerful voice, "I ran into that Ben kid earlier. He said you'd gone inside because you weren't feeling well."

Her fists clenched at the words "that Ben," but she should probably let it go, since they weren't getting together. "Yeah. Headache."

She went to the refrigerator and pulled out turkey, lettuce, tomatoes, and spicy mustard. She skipped the cheese, though. Faux-cheddar didn't make anyone's day better. "Can I have a mini fridge in my room?"

Her dad made a choking sound, and she turned to look at him over her shoulder. He wasn't strangling on his arugula—he was laughing. "Disappointed in what you found in ours?"

She put her hands on her hips. "Aren't you? I swear I won't tell Mom."

"I'm very glad she looks after our health." He smiled. "But I do wish she'd let me drink something other than lite beer. I'd kill for a Newcastle Brown right now."

She sat at the table with him and waggled her eyebrows. "If you buy me a mini fridge, I'll hide better beer for you."

"Nice try." His smile faded. "Is everything okay? You've been so down the last week or so. You can talk to me, you know."

Sure, she could. *Hey Daddy, I'm not sure I want to be a doctor or go to your alma mater. I might want to go to Baylor and crush all your dreams.* No—that wasn't a conversation she was ready to have. "Stress. That's all."

"But, Pea, there's no reason for a seventeen-year-old girl

to be *this* stressed." He reached across the table to squeeze her hand. "Tell me what's wrong."

Her lower lip quivered with the effort of holding back tears. Damn it, she was crying way too much these days. "You wouldn't understand."

"Yesterday I had to explain to a healthy fifty-two-year-old man that he had early onset Alzheimer's. I doubt you'll tell me anything worse than that."

Could she tell him? Could she *really?* His job was so hard…but his expression was so kind. Maybe he'd understand after all—and if he did, she wouldn't have to keep beating her head against the wall in calculus.

She wouldn't have to keep beating her head against the wall over Ben.

The thought of breaking off their arrangement caused a dull ache to form behind her breastbone. At the very least, she owed him help with Zoey, and she couldn't leave him hanging. But did that mean she couldn't take one step for herself? She was so tired of making everyone else's life better at her own expense.

"Honey, tell me," Daddy said. "Please?"

How could she tell him about med school, when she didn't know for sure? Still, she *was* sure about one thing. Maybe it was time to tell him. "I'm… It's… Okay, what if I told you I didn't want to go to Stanford?"

The color drained from his face. "But we'd already decided you would."

"First, that assumes they accept my application," she said, anger flooding her chest, replacing the ache. "And second, that's what *you* decided."

"No, I'm pretty sure we decided together." He shoved

his chair back from the table, a surprised—hurt—look on his face. "This is very important to me, yes, because I know what kind of education they offer. Only the best for my daughter."

"But I can get a perfectly good undergrad education in Texas, Daddy." She hated how her voice shook and hated even more that she cried when she was mad. It made Daddy feel guilty, and that's not what she wanted. Worse, to Mom, it signaled weakness. "There are great schools here. Please, don't make me go so far away."

He had a finger raised, ready to point it at her, so when he paused, it remained suspended. After a moment, he lowered his hand and closed his mouth. When he finally met her eyes, he looked hurt. "Is that what's wrong? You'd be homesick?"

"Partly, yes." She wiped her nose on a napkin. It wasn't time to tell him the rest. If he wigged out this much over her not going to Stanford, he'd lose it if she told him she had doubts about studying medicine. "I like Texas."

He was quiet for a long while, and she was struck by the gray hair peppering the stubble on his chin. Her daddy wasn't supposed to grow old. He worked out, ate right—he was supposed to endure forever. But that wasn't true, was it?

A cold prickle stole down her neck. If she didn't follow in his footsteps, his practice would close or be sold to another doctor. Worse, he wouldn't live out his dream of working with her, teaching her his trade. How could she hurt him like that? And how would she feel if he found another young doctor to mentor instead? Horrible. That's how she'd feel.

The weight of a thousand expectations fell on her back. She couldn't do this to him. "If it means that much to you, I'll go to Stanford. Assuming I'm accepted."

"No," he said quickly. "No, Pea, no. I hate the idea of you going so far away, too, to tell the truth. Besides, Rice and Baylor are both exceptional private schools for our field. We can find you a good fit closer to home."

His smile was both relieved and reassuring, so Paige forced herself to smile back. "Okay. I applied to Baylor, so I'll just...go apply to Rice."

"Good. But don't let up on your studies, okay? Both those schools are very competitive, especially Rice." He stood and went to the sink. "So, whatever you have going on with that Ben? Maybe you should keep it strictly about school."

Numb, she murmured, "There's nothing going on with Ben."

"Good. There's plenty of time for that later. Find a nice guy in med school—another doctor in the family would be a plus. Especially another neuro. I could leave the practice to both of you. That way, I wouldn't have to sell my practice when I retire. It would stay ours, and keep all our good work in the family." He came to kiss her on top of the head, then left her alone with her boring sandwich and hollow future.

Paige rested her head on her folded arms. Not only did he still expect her to become a doctor...

...now he expected her to marry one.

Chapter Twenty-Four

BEN

The theater had been a mess all night. The main popcorn machine broke, some kid slipped on a soft-drink spill, and the projector in Theater Two kept hanging up during the previews. The assistant manager, Lily, yelled at anybody and everybody for three straight hours because that's what she did when she freaked out.

And, yet, Ben had never been happier to be so busy, because he didn't have time to worry about how mad Paige would be at him for snapping at her dad. Instead, he could focus on fighting with the popcorn machine. Being the resident mechanic, that was almost always his job. When he fixed it just as the nine o'clock rush hit, people actually cheered and Lily stopped yelling at everyone. Here, at the Alderwood Eight, he was a hero.

The feeling didn't last long. When he went to clock out

in the break room at ten thirty, he finally checked his phone and blew out a breath. No messages. Was Paige ignoring him? Giving him the silent treatment?

He couldn't decide whether to text her or leave it alone until some time had passed. They weren't on to study tomorrow, which meant he didn't have to see her until Monday. But he wasn't working tomorrow, either—how would he make it through a whole empty day if he didn't hear from her?

"Thanks again for the popcorn machine," Lily called.

"No problem." He paused. "Can I ask a really weird question?"

"You can ask fourteen weird questions. You're the Popcorn Man." She smiled. It was the first time he'd seen her smile all night. "What's up?"

This was awkward, but she was a senior at UNT and he'd overheard her talk to a lot of guys over the last two years. "So, there's this girl."

"Ooh, I like this question already. Here, let me get comfy." She leaned against the wall, her expression captivated. "Please, continue."

He gave her the side-eye but said, "She's in a tough spot with her dad, and this morning, I kind of blew up at him for being an asshole and may have accidentally made him ask her some tough questions. She hasn't texted me yet, and I don't know what that means. Is she mad? Should I text and find out how she is?"

"Ah, young love." Lily grinned. "I forgot how messy high school was."

"You know what? Never mind. Thanks anyway," Ben said. He slid his ID through the card reader to clock out, and turned to go.

"Wait. I was just reminiscing." She put a hand on his arm to stop him from opening the door. "I remember how hard all this stuff is—and guys always try to figure out girls without actually talking to them, which usually backfires and ends up with you being screamed at in the senior hallway. So, text her. Before Monday."

He scratched his head. Was it really that simple? "That's it? Text her?"

"Yes, dumbass. Ask her if she's okay. That's it—don't elaborate. If she's pissed at you, you'll know." Something metallic clattered out front in the concession stand. "I need to go crack heads. Tell me how it went, okay? I love a good soap opera."

She pushed the door open, yelling, "Who dropped the popcorn basket? So help me, it's like working in a zoo!"

Chuckling, Ben pushed the back door open and went to his bike before he could catch the rest of her tirade. Text Paige. That was logical—so why was it so hard?

He set his backpack down on the concrete and pulled out his phone. His fingers were shaking. Why did she make him so crazy? Why was it he always wanted what he couldn't have? He wanted a car—that wasn't going to happen. He'd thought he wanted Zoey. His chances were better there, but still a long shot.

That's when it hit him. He wanted Paige—he knew that much. But…even if they started something, he still couldn't have her, not for long. She was on one path, off to Stanford and probably med school, and he was on another, off to A&M and engineering conferences. For a short while, the paths converged, but they'd split very soon. It was a completely hopeless deal.

He stuck his phone in his backpack and rode home.

Mom was waiting up for him, watching old movies and eating popcorn. "Want some?" she asked, holding up the bowl.

"If I never see popcorn again, I'll be entirely happy." He tossed his backpack onto a kitchen chair. "I'm going to bed."

"Hey, wait a sec." Mom set down her bowl and patted the sofa cushion next to her. "Talk to me?"

He stood in the kitchen, not sure whether to run for his room or do as she asked. If he sat on that couch, everything would come bubbling out, and he didn't want to worry her with his crap.

"Benjamin, come here," she said, patting the cushion.

Heaving a big sigh, he went to sit. "I'm tired."

"I can see that. And I hate how hard you have to work." She ruffled his hair, smiling. "The haircut's growing on me."

"Me, too."

"This have something to do with the girl we talked about last night?"

"'This' what?"

She turned off the TV. "The mopey face."

"This is my regular long-day-slash-after-work face."

"I've been your mother close to eighteen years—I'm like the Snow White of your seven different expressions. I can read them all. And you, son, are Mopey Face."

"Okay, fine. Yes, it's the girl. I think I upset her."

"That's easy to fix," Mom said. "Apologizing always works."

He snorted. "It would if I knew for sure she was mad. But, see, if I apologize, and she's not mad, she might *get* mad."

Mom gave him a blank look. "I didn't follow a word of

that."

"It's okay. I'll figure it out."

He left her with her black-and-white movies and went to his room. Why had he asked Paige to agree to this crazy plan? He should've known, in the first ten seconds after they met, that she would plow ahead until she succeeded in setting him up with Zoey. She was just that kind of girl. She got things done, no matter how weird the request was.

After taking a shower, he changed into a pair of shorts to sleep in and went to bed. A little light from the moon and one of the working streetlights filtered in under his curtains. If he slept, everything would be clear in the morning. He hoped so, anyway. Except he couldn't sleep. He needed to do something, anything, even if it was all wrong. So, he'd text Paige.

He was reaching for his phone when it buzzed on his nightstand. He snatched it up, hoping to see Paige's name on the screen.

Instead, it was a number he didn't recognize.

Ben? Hi, it's Zoey Miller.

Chapter Twenty-Five

Paige spent most of Sunday morning in her room. The beautiful blue sky called to her from her window, begging her to come out for a swim and some sun. Instead, she was wrapping up the last pieces of her application to Rice. She'd need to line up her counselor and teacher recommendations next week, but she had until January 1 to turn it all in, so she didn't have to panic. Not about this, anyway. Besides, she didn't have the energy to worry about it much. She hadn't slept well, and when she had, she dreamed of marrying a man whose face was a blur. They were both wearing long white doctor's coats over their wedding clothes. Daddy was wearing his, too, and her mother was dressed head-to-toe in Chanel.

She'd woken up in a cold sweat.

Worst of all, Zoey still hadn't texted her back. Part of her wanted to text, to see what was up, but she couldn't bring herself to ask. What if Zoey said, *Oh, yeah, Ben's so my type. Fix me up and let me hit that*?

Paige would probably spend the rest of the day hiding under the covers.

For the same reason, she didn't want to text Ben. He had the day off for once, and she didn't want to bother him. He had a lot to do, and none of it involved her, at least today. He was going his way, and she was going hers.

She tapped her fingers on her desk, staring at her completed application. What if she and Ben weren't going separate ways, though? Staying in Texas would mean they weren't so far apart, especially if she went to Rice. What would she do with her life then? Would this first step give her the courage to think about a new career? And maybe telling Ben how she felt?

She thought of Mr. Kennedy at the ElderCare center. Of piano-playing Mrs. Ybarra. Of how happy a little attention and love made them feel. And how giving them that attention and love made *her* feel. Maybe she could still have that, even if she was a doctor. She just had to find a way.

Hope blossomed in her chest, and she got an idea. Quickly, Paige threw a sweater over her tank top and shoved her feet into a pair of flip-flops. She needed to try something.

On her way out, she passed her parents in the kitchen. They were eating whole grain English muffins and poached eggs.

"Just a suggestion," she said, reaching for a banana as she flew by. "Poached food is nasty."

Daddy let out his weird, half-strangled laugh, while Mom said, "It is not!"

"Dear, let's face it," Daddy said, just before Paige closed the door to the garage. "It really is."

Feeling lighter, she jumped into the Mustang, noticing after the fact how *clean* it was. Ben had finished washing it for her. A rush of affection raced through her veins. All the more reason to keep moving.

She made it to the ElderCare center just as they were serving lunch. Meals were held early here, and everyone was settled in the dining hall when she came in at eleven fifteen. The round tables were full of residents, some eating on their own, some being assisted. No fewer than a dozen heads turned at her entrance, and more than half smiled in recognition. The others were further gone, but they still looked at her with pleasant curiosity.

Smiling in return, Paige checked with Mrs. Cardell, the dining hall manager. "Can I serve dessert today? I haven't been here much this week and I missed my peeps."

Mrs. Cardell gave her a big hug. She was a soft, round lady, and it was like hugging a rose-scented pillow. "Honey, I would love that. The cart is already loaded if you want to take it around."

Paige checked it out. Green Jell-O, chocolate cake, and lemon bars were the choices today. "Can I have a piece of cake when I'm done?"

"Knowing your mama's idea of dessert, I'll hold back two pieces," Mrs. Cardell said. "No teenager goes sugar-free in my kitchen."

"I do love you, you know."

"Sure do. Now, get the cart rolling before our friends start a revolt."

Paige made her way through the dining hall, passing

out dessert, reminding people they could only pick one, and making sure each resident received a compliment or kind word. It was wonderful to see how the atmosphere changed. Even the most advanced patients were calmer, and everyone seemed happier, more content.

She stood up tall, pleased—she could bring smiles to people who sometimes forgot how. So many of them were wary of doctors, though. How could she reassure them and brighten their day, if she was the "mean one" forcing them to lie down in front of the CT scanner?

She sighed. This wasn't the time to worry about this stuff. She was here to spread a little fun—worrying could wait an hour.

After her rounds, she sought out Mrs. Ybarra and took her to the piano. "I'm playing in a recital. Could I play for you?"

Mrs. Ybarra patted her shoulder. Her long gray hair was pulled back in a knot at the back of her neck, and a pair of glasses hung on a bright pink lanyard clipped to her shirt. Her eyes crinkled as she smiled. "Oh, Pamela. That's my good girl, practicing so hard."

Pamela was Mrs. Ybarra's daughter, but it didn't bother her to be confused with someone Mrs. Ybarra loved so much. Paige nodded. "I have been, ma'am."

The nurses helped bring more patients into the salon as she prepared to play. Once they had a full house, she warmed up with a few scales—to applause, which was adorable—then started the Beethoven. She stumbled on the allegro again but righted herself quickly and finished well. More applause, especially from Mrs. Ybarra, who had happy tears streaming down her face.

She could do better than this, right? She switched to a Joplin rag her piano teacher had made her learn last year, and all the residents started clapping and tapping their feet. She played and played, for more than an hour, until she started to run out of pieces she had memorized. She ended with "Danny Boy," and there wasn't a dry eye once Nurse Smith began singing along.

Paige felt like she might explode with joy, and her throat grew tight. They were so *happy*. Because of her. Not because she solved their problems or finished their projects, but because she cared. She wanted to do this every day, just to see them smile.

The director of the center had arrived while she was playing, and he offered to walk her out after she'd made it — hugged, kissed, patted — through the crowd of patients.

Dr. Geldman was a big man, with a craggy face and thinning gray hair. He made Paige feel tiny as they walked to the main entrance. Outside, the tree branches swayed in a stiff breeze and the sunlight warmed the small lobby where they stopped to talk.

"You have a gift for this," he said. "Caring for the elderly. Music therapy is a big key to their treatment, and you nailed it."

"Thank you, sir," she said, beaming. To hear a professional say she belonged in a place like this, helping people deal with tough times, was encouraging. "I like it here."

"I know you're planning to become a neurologist, but if you ever change your mind, come see me. I'd love to talk to you about geriatrics. It's a growing field, what with all the Boomers entering into retirement age. We need young talent like you, people with the 'touch,' as I like to say. You have a compassionate heart, Miss Westfield. The residents instinctively know you're here to care for them."

For once, things started to make sense. What if she didn't become a neurologist? What if she studied another field — geriatrics or psychology — something that would help these people as much as a doctor...or maybe even more?

She nodded. "I'll think about it. And thank you for telling me — it's nice to hear I'm good at this."

"You certainly are."

She shook his hand, then practically skipped to the Mustang. It was such a beautiful, perfect day. She was figuring out what she wanted to do with her life, and it was surprising how her stress melted away when she considered it. She'd think on it a few days, while she thought about how to explain all this to Daddy. Mom wouldn't be happy, but for once, Paige needed to do what was right for her, even if it violated their carefully laid plans.

Excited, she decided to stop at Main Street Diner and pick up some lunch. She'd save her cake for later — right now, she wanted sweet potato fries and a cheeseburger. No poached food for her today.

Maybe not ever again.

Chapter Twenty-Six

BEN

"So, tell the truth now," Zoey said, stirring her milkshake with her straw. "I bought you Sunday brunch at the fabulous Main Street Diner and sat through a really long explanation to a really simple question. You owe me."

Ben found it amusing that she liked strawberry shakes. There was something so odd about watching someone drink pink milk, but it was Zoey, and she could make anything look good. "Okay, okay. You're right. I like her."

"I knew it!" She pumped a fist in the air. "Paige likes you, too."

"What? No. No, she really doesn't." He squirmed on his barstool, uncomfortable. He'd grudgingly let Zoey know about his arrangement with Paige—painful, especially since Zoey had looked a little furious at being set up—but now they were skating into foreign territory. "I'm helping her with calculus, that's all."

"Uh-huh." She took a sip of milkshake and Ben felt, rather than saw, every guy under the age of thirty watch her with that straw.

Funny enough, it didn't affect him as it would've a few weeks ago. When she'd texted him last night, he'd definitely had mixed feelings about it. Then when she'd said she wanted to talk about Paige, she had his attention, and he'd agreed to this lunch. It was kind of strange to have a girl he barely knew take him out for a hamburger, but she claimed it was for her friend, so he decided to trust her.

"No, seriously. She's told me a bunch of times about how she had her future all mapped out, and it doesn't sound like there's room for me—or anything else, to be honest—in her plans."

Zoey rolled her baby-blue eyes, and the fry cook dropped his spatula. She gave him a concerned look and he flashed her a hopeful smile.

"Okay, honestly," Ben said. "Do you even notice that every guy in a five-mile radius is dying to prove his love for you?"

She sighed. "They think I'm pretty. So what? They don't know me."

"Yeah, but I know you...a little anyway, and I think you're nice."

She blew a raspberry, and Ben burst out laughing. "I am nice, *sometimes*," she said, "but these guys don't care about that. They just see the wrapping paper, and that's not the kind of guy I'm looking for."

Her tone was sharp and uninviting. What was she hiding? Because he suddenly had this idea that Zoey knew exactly what—and who—she wanted but wasn't planning to let him in on the secret. "I'm just impressed is all, because I have the opposite problem—it takes an act of God for a girl to notice me."

Zoey snickered. "Like stripping off your shirt while washing a car? Nice abs, by the way."

Good thing they weren't sitting closer, because he flushed hot enough to melt her milkshake. That scene made him look either desperate or like a douche unless he spilled how Paige had tricked him into it. He wouldn't, though. "Um…yeah. It was, uh, warm out."

"I'll say."

"So, now that you know the truth about Paige and me," he said, hoping to change the subject, "what are you going to do with it?"

She pushed her milkshake glass aside and turned on her barstool to face him. "First thing I'm going to do is ask you what you *want* me to do with it."

He stared blankly at her. "Like what?"

"Do you want me to tell her? Play matchmaker? Or do you want me to forget I know?" She frowned. "I can't. Forget, I mean. Because I really, *really* want to see you two together."

Irony was a bitch, but he was cautiously hopeful. "You do?"

"Yeah. You're perfect for her. And she obviously likes you."

"You keep saying that," he said. "But I just don't see it."

"Only one way to find out—tell her." She raised one perfect blond eyebrow and something clattered in the kitchen. The poor fry cook yelped. Zoey groaned and glanced in his direction. "Really?"

The guy practically ducked behind the counter, and Ben chuckled. "He's a senior at Alderwood. His name is Adam — I know him from physics. He's probably lost all motor control from sheer proximity. Hell, he probably lost a finger."

"Ridiculous." She picked up her milkshake. "So anyway, do you want to tell Paige? Or do you want me to do it? Girl gossip is a powerful tool, my friend."

If Zoey told Paige he was interested, would she cut things off? That was a pretty big risk. "I don't know…"

"Look, there are all kinds of reasons this is more complicated than it should be. She likes you. You like her. It shouldn't be so hard, but it is." Her expression told him that she had experience with this somehow. "I want Paige to be happy. Because she's not, and she hasn't been in a while. She's always doing her damnedest to make everyone else happy instead, and I'll tell you why if you're ready to hear it."

"I'm ready," he said, riveted by what she said — Zoey knew her friend better than Paige realized.

"All her life, her parents have pushed her to be a 'good little achiever.' Especially her mom. Man, she's the picture next to the definition for Type A. My parents? They couldn't give a crap how I do in school, as long as I'm not suspended for anything stupid, which is kind of liberating in its own way. How about yours?"

"Parent, singular. My mom. She gives a crap, but she's pretty great about it."

Zoey pounded a fist on the table. "See? My parentals have no expectations. Your mom sounds like she has expectations, but they're about you, am I right?" He nodded and she did, too. "Paige's parents want her to follow The Plan.

Her mom controls every morsel of food in that house. And speaking of the house? It's spotless, all the time. I've never seen a dirty dish in the sink. Not once, and I stay overnight often enough to notice. It's nuts how much of a control freak Mrs. W. can be. She cares about Paige, but she's wound *way* too tight and ends up smothering her kid. Her dad, he's nice enough, but he's a dad—they can be kind of blind to the fact that their daughters don't want to live life according to their rules."

"I can see that," he said.

"She's so wrapped up in what they expect of her, she can't cut loose and let herself be close to anybody. Trust me, I tried to fix her up with some great guys after her last boyfriend. Nothing. She wasn't interested."

His heart plummeted. "If it hasn't worked before, why will it work now?"

"I'm not promising it will work," she said kindly. She laid her hand on his arm and motioned him to lean closer. "I'm saying it's worth a shot, because you're the first guy she's shown any real interest in. In fact, she's shown more interest in you than she did in Caleb—and she dated him for months."

"So what do we do?" he asked, hardly able to believe what Zoey was saying.

"Oh, come on, Franklin, work with me."

Bewildered, he shook his head. "No idea."

She laughed. "Okay, so first we—" Zoey darted a look out the window. "Oh, shit."

And there was Paige. She was staring at the two of them, cozied up at the table, with her mouth open and deep hurt in her eyes. She turned and started running away from the diner.

A bolt of ice crashed through him, shocking him to the core. Ben's first instinct was to leap up and run after her. Zoey's hand locked onto his arm. "No! Leave this to me. She won't believe you if you say it's nothing. She might believe me."

He'd put so much faith in Paige, and now Zoey—and nothing had gone right. "What makes you think you'll do any better at fixing this than I would?"

"Because," she snapped. "And that's all I'm going to say. Go home, and keep your phone handy. I'll text you later with plans."

She grabbed her purse and swept from the diner before Ben could even stand. He watched her run by in the direction Paige had gone. How badly did karma hate him?

He had no idea if Zoey could fix things. Maybe it was time he started making his own plans instead of trusting them to someone else.

Chapter Twenty-Seven

PAIGE

Paige couldn't breathe. Couldn't think. Ben was having lunch at a little table by the window…with Zoey. Her hand had been on his arm, and they were laughing, their heads angled toward each other.

All her happiness had drained away in a flash, leaving her hands clammy and her heart aching. She ran back to her car, gasping for air. God, oh God. She was too late—they'd already started seeing each other. Ben and Zoey had become a "thing," and Paige had done barely anything to make it happen.

But…she'd thought….

Tears rolled down her face. No, whatever she'd thought about Ben, about how he might feel about her, it was dead-ass wrong.

Paige fumbled with her keys, unlocked her car door, and

wrenched it open. She had to get out of here. She needed some air and a place to hide from everyone and everything. She couldn't un-see what she just saw, and it was going to take some time to put herself back together.

She peeled out of the parking lot in time to see Zoey jogging down the sidewalk. She was waving her arms, mouthing, "Stop! Wait!"

Screw that. She was hauling ass out of here before Ben could see she was upset. He'd had a lunch date with Zoey—without letting her know, that bastard—and she couldn't mess that up for him. It was bad enough that Zoey had seen her face and realized she was upset.

She gunned the engine and shot down Main Street at ten over the speed limit. How could she have let herself get in so deep? Swiping tears from her cheeks, she missed a stop sign and cruised straight through an intersection. Seconds later, red and blue lights flashed in her rearview mirror.

She pulled over to the curb and buried her face in her hands. How did this day go from so hopeful to so hopeless in the space of five minutes?

The officer knocked on her window and she lowered it. "I know, Officer. I know I ran it." She fished her license out of her purse and reached to pull her registration out of the glove box. "I'm sorry."

The policeman, who appeared to be in his mid-forties, stared at her with concern. "Miss, are you all right?"

She slumped farther down in her seat. "Everyone keeps asking me that."

He smiled a little. "Sounds like you aren't, then. You said you knew you ran the stop sign. I can only assume you were crying and didn't see it?"

Paige nodded, feeling like the world's biggest idiot, especially when she caught Zoey's BMW easing up behind the police cruiser.

"I have a sixteen-year-old daughter, so I know a little about this kind of thing. If you promise that you'll do the speed limit the whole way home—and *go* straight home—I'll let you off with a warning. Agreed?"

She swiped the tears from her cheeks. "Agreed. Thank you, sir."

He scribbled something on his notepad, then tore off a section for her. Underlined in the comments section was, *Needs a nap and some ice cream.*

He had no idea.

She waited for him to pull away before starting her car. As the officer asked, she drove straight home, obeying all traffic laws—and the BMW kept pace behind her the whole freaking way. When she pulled into her driveway, Zoey stopped at the curb and hopped out.

"I'm not in the mood to talk, Zoey," she mumbled, holding out a hand. "I need to be alone right now. Please, just go home. Or better yet, go find Ben and…and…"

Zoey looked like she might cry, too. "Girl, you don't even know how to finish that sentence, do you? And you know why?"

"Not sure I care anymore," Paige said, turning toward the house. Every bone in her body ached, almost like she had the flu. Could you be so heartsick that it made you physically ill? Why hadn't she said something to Ben before it was too late?

Jogging footsteps pounded up the drive, and Zoey darted in front of her to block her path. "I'm going to tell you anyway. You can't finish that sentence because Ben and me? We're just friends. Whatever you thought you saw, all we were doing was having lunch."

She shook her head. "Girls don't 'just have lunch' with guys they barely know unless they like them."

"Oh, really?" Zoey crossed her arms. "So, tell me something, Miss I Don't Need a Boyfriend, I Have Stanford. Why are you so pissed with me? Yesterday, you said he was just a friend, and you seemed really interested in how I felt about him. If that were true, you'd be asking me how lunch went, not speeding off like a banshee and getting a ticket."

A vein started throbbing in Paige's forehead. "Of course I like him!"

Zoey threw up her hands. "See? Was that so hard to admit? It's obvious you like him a lot."

"And it doesn't matter, because he likes you, just like every other boy I know. I'm always second best. Always." She took a few heaving breaths. "Beautiful Zoey or Perfect, Type-A Paige—who would want me when you're in the universe?"

A shocked silence closed in around them, then Zoey pulled her into a hug. "Who would want you rather than me? Lots of guys would, but how about just one? I had lunch with Ben today to talk about you."

"Me?" she mumbled. "What about me?"

"He told me something kind of interesting." Zoey stepped back. "Want to grab a drink and go sit by the pool?"

Paige nodded, and they raided the fridge for diet sodas and a basket of fresh strawberries. "Best I can do," she said meekly.

Zoey laughed, her eyes wide. "You actually have Diet

Dr Pepper? Real Diet Dr Pepper, not that Stevia knock-off from Whole Foods?"

"I think it was a blue moon the day Mom went to the store," Paige said, smiling a little. "Or she was possessed. Doesn't matter which—I'm not complaining."

They went out onto the patio, and the ceiling fans dried Paige's cheeks. She had no idea what was going on here, but hope was starting to creep back into her vocabulary.

Zoey opened her soda and took a long drink before saying, "So, what's this about you setting Ben up with me?"

Paige's eyes popped open wide. "What? I… What?"

He'd told her? Why? *Why* would he do that? What was wrong with him? You didn't tell the girl you were trying to go out with that her best friend was fixing you up unless… "Oh."

"Yeah. 'Oh.'" She laughed. "You know me. Have you seen me date a single guy at Alderwood in the last two years, except as friends?"

Paige frowned. "No. I just thought that was because you preferred more mature guys."

"And so you decided to turn Ben into something you *assumed* I'd like?"

She focused on her soda can. "It meant a lot to him. And I'm…I'm flunking calc, okay?"

Zoey nodded slowly. "I knew something was wrong. Why didn't you tell me? There's no shame in having a hard time in class. It happens to most of us, you know." Her foot nudged at Paige's ankle. "Not everyone can be perfect all the time. It's too hard."

And here she'd thought people would laugh and be meanly happy she was a failure. "I should've told you. I was just…too ashamed, I guess. Anyway, Ben found out, and he's a genius and offered to help. In exchange, he wanted a chance to get your attention."

"He got my attention all right. About the time I caught *you* staring open-mouthed at his chest during that little car wash yesterday," Zoey said. "Is he cute? Yes. Is he sweet? Definitely. But you don't actually know if I have a thing for cute, sweet math geeks. Maybe I like skaters, or pro wrestlers, or guitarists in garage bands. You have no idea, right?"

She shook her head. "I just assumed…"

"You and the rest of Alderwood. Let me handle my love life, okay? Oh, and the reason I asked you all those questions about him yesterday is because I wanted to find out who he was so I could put the two of you together. I see how you look at each other, even if you're both totally oblivious. I didn't assume—I observed and came to a scientifically accurate conclusion. Did you even see how clean your car is? He's bending over backward to impress you. Not me. *You.*"

A dozen emotions were warring for control in Paige's mind: joy, fear, excitement, doubt. She settled on apologetic— it seemed safest at the moment. "I'm really sorry for thinking I could set you up without telling you what we were doing."

"Thank you for that. Now, you have some thinking to do."

"About what?"

Zoey rolled her eyes and stood. "Ben, silly. B-E-N. Now that you know he likes you, don't you think you should, I don't know, do something about it?"

She hesitated. "My parents—"

"To hell with them," Zoey snapped with more force than Paige expected. "They aren't allowed to choose your heart.

You were so quick to make over Ben, but you really need to make over your own life instead. Hear me? This time *you choose*."

She swung her hair over her shoulder and marched out of the backyard, looking like a runway model with each step. She was right about one thing—well, she was right about a lot of things—Paige had some thinking to do.

It was time to decide for sure who she wanted to be, and it had to be for *her* and not anyone else.

Chapter Twenty-Eight

Ben

Ben rode home as hard as his body would allow, and he was soaking wet by the time he got there. He leaned against the house after parking his bike, panting and shaking with frustration. Of all the stinking bad luck. He'd finally figured things out, and a stupid misunderstanding had ruined it all.

Mom opened the side door, carrying a trash bag. When she saw him, she shrieked and jumped. "You scared me! What are you doing out here?"

"Nothing," he said, wiping the sweat off his forehead. "Nothing at all."

She took the bag to the trash can, then came back and peered at his face. "Please tell me you apologized to that girl."

"Not even close. It's complicated, but I made things ten

times worse completely by accident."

"Then I guess you'd better come in and have a cookie." She led him inside and gestured at the kitchen counter. It was covered with pans and plates and boxes of cookies—three different kinds. "Too much time on my hands and a sale on flour that was about to expire. There's dough in the freezer, too."

At least one thing was staying constant. He could always rely on being fed, no matter how bad their situation was. He grabbed a chocolate chip. "Have you ever thought about doing this? Selling cookies? Because these are really good."

"Eh, maybe. There hasn't been much time to think about it, though." She pointed at the kitchen table. "Sit. Let's hear it."

It took nearly twenty minutes to tell her the whole thing—from the moment he saw Paige take a flying dive to the floor at school, all the way up to her catching him with Zoey, and Zoey running after her.

"So she said to wait, and to trust her." He shook his head. "Seems like I should do something myself."

"Do you like Paige enough to grovel?" Mom asked, with a shrewd glance at the kitchen.

"I like her enough to grovel, yeah."

She smiled. "Then I have an idea. And my ideas you definitely can trust—because they involve cookies."

After she explained, Ben went to take a quick shower while Mom fixed up a gift box for Paige. She'd been right—this was a good way to go. What do you give a girl who has everything, including a health-nut mother? You give her the one thing she can't have: cookies.

When he was done and dressed in the dark jeans and

blue T-shirt, fresh from the Laundromat, he took the box and the car keys from Mom.

"Drive carefully," she said, picking a piece of lint from his collar. "And be home by ten. You need your sleep."

"Yes, Ma. And thanks."

It was almost four by the time he pulled into Paige's neighborhood in his mom's ten-year-old Buick. People outside took some double takes at the car, but he didn't care. For once he was going to show up somewhere without looking like he'd walked through a windy oven.

Paige's car was in the driveway when he parked at the curb in front of her house. Nobody was outside. He took a deep breath, picked up the box, and walked to her door. The doorbell sounded like a Chinese gong signaling someone's execution. Probably his.

A moment later, Mrs. Westfield called, "I'll get it."

Great—he had to pass the Mom test upfront. When the door swung open, he swallowed hard and said, "May I speak to Paige, please?"

Mrs. Westfield stared at him for a long moment. "Why?"

Every atom in his body wanted him to say, *None of your business*, but he reined it in. "Because I owe her an apology. I, uh, brought her something."

"Who is it?" Dr. Westfield asked, coming up behind his wife. "Ah, hello, Ben."

"Hi, sir. Um, any chance I can see Paige? I'm afraid her gift is going to melt."

Mrs. Westfield's gaze narrowed. "Melt?"

"Melt?" Dr. Westfield asked, sounding hopeful. "What'cha got there? Ice cream?"

Mrs. Westfield turned her glare on him and he held up

his hands. "Let the kid in, Diana. He's fine."

He's fine? He'd snapped at the guy yesterday afternoon. Hadn't Dr. Westfield asked Paige about being a doctor and found out she didn't know if she wanted to be one? He was so confused—what did he need to apologize for now? Two things? One? "Please, Mrs. Westfield. It'll only take a minute, then I'll leave if that's what you want."

Her expression softened. "Phil tells me you're pretty bright. What are you planning to study after high school?"

What, did he have to pass an interview to go in? "Engineering. Mechanical Engineering to be precise." There, stuffy vocabulary words ought to help. "I like figuring out how things work and making them work better."

"Except girls. There's no way to figure out how they work," Dr. Westfield muttered under his breath, then shot Ben an amused look before calling out, "Paige! You have a guest!"

Mrs. Westfield sighed but opened the door wider to let him through. "Please come in."

"Easier for us to grill you in here," Dr. Westfield added, looking like he might laugh at any second. Ben was starting to like him, even if he was forcing Paige to follow in his footsteps. Except now he could totally see why she couldn't bring herself to disappoint him. This was a guy who made you hope he approved of you.

Footsteps sounded on the stairs, then stopped abruptly. Ben looked up and froze. Paige had paused midstep, her eyes wide with surprise. She also looked so beautiful. Since lunchtime, she'd pulled her hair up, exposing her long, smooth neck. And where did that sundress come from? So. Much. Leg. And skin. Miles and miles of skin. He had to clench the cookie box to keep his hands from shaking from wanting to touch her.

Dr. Westfield cleared his throat noisily. "I think your mother and I are going to the living room to watch a movie," he said in a cheerful, loud voice. "Why don't you kids go out to the patio? Don't make the young man wait, honey."

Paige's face was flushed, and Ben's heart started to race. One of them needed to move, otherwise her parents were going to have a complete meltdown. He held out the box. "I brought you a present."

She stayed where she was, blinking so that her eyelashes fluttered. "You did?"

"Yes," her dad called. "He did. Why don't you come down here and find out what it is. I can smell chocolate, and if you don't take it, I will. And I might even kiss him if there're cookies in that box."

Mrs. Westfield rolled her eyes. "There's no need to threaten bodily harm on a teenager for your sweet tooth."

They walked away, arguing about grocery lists that included Newcastle Brown and big slabs of steak. That seemed to break the spell that held Paige in place on the stairs, and she came down slowly. He watched every move, drinking her in. Wishing he could kiss every inch of exposed skin… and some that wasn't exposed, too.

"You're here," she murmured, not meeting his eyes. "I was scared that…"

"That what?"

"That you might be mad at me. Because I've been kind of bitchy the last few days."

"God, Paige," he said. "No, I'm not mad at you. I thought for sure you'd be mad at *me*."

She shook her head. "I'm not. How could I be? But can I still have whatever's in that box?"

"Only if you take me outside where we can be alone."

She smiled shyly, then slipped her hand into his. Her hand was so soft, and he held it gently, rubbing his thumb along her wrist as she led him to the back door. He smiled when he saw the goose bumps on her arm.

"I would ask to sit in your lap again, but I think my parents might be paying more attention this time," she said.

His entire body went hot, then cold, then hot again. "Maybe next time."

She laughed. "Maybe so."

They sat side-by-side on a porch swing at the far end of the patio. Her leg was warm against his, and he could feel himself sliding toward her, dying to touch more than just her hand. Not trusting himself to speak, he gave her the box.

She had to let go of his hand to open it, and he missed it right away. He held his breath as she checked out the cookies, then held up the note, silently asking if she could read it. He nodded, and she opened it. She took his hand as she read it, tears brimming at the edge of her eyelashes. When she finished, she set the note back in the box and put it on a side table.

"Do you mean it?" she whispered. "What you said on the card?"

You're the only girl in the room, he'd written. "Yes. I mean it." He slid his arm around her shoulders and pulled her closer. "When you're in the room, I can't see anything — or anyone — else. Only you."

"Why didn't you tell me before now?" she asked.

"Same reason you didn't tell me — and still haven't." He

smiled when her head jerked up so she could stare at him. "Because I thought there was no way you'd like me. Does that tell you something? I held you to a higher standard than Zoey. I thought I was good enough for her, but…Paige, I knew there was no way I'd ever be good enough for you, because you're amazing and beautiful and smart and funny—"

"And I thought I wasn't good enough for you," she murmured.

"I don't even know how," he whispered, planting a kiss on top of her head. "So…do you know how I feel about you now? Because I'll say it a thousand different ways if I have to."

"And I'd love to hear them all." She scooted over so that their faces were only inches apart. "But we're still going in different directions."

"Not right now," he whispered, resting his cheek against her temple so he could breathe in the smell of her hair. "And I'm tired of waiting for what I want to come true. I'm ready to have some of my future right now."

"It's not so easy for me," she said into his collarbone. "But I can try."

"All I wanted to hear." He tilted her face up to his. "I'm going to kiss you, Paige Westfield."

"Please do, Ben Franklin."

When their lips met, she sighed against his mouth, and the sound lit a fire in his chest. Ignoring the prospect that her parents might be watching, he pulled her into his lap and wrapped his arms around her. She cradled his face in her hands as their mouths moved together, exploring. His head swam from lack of air, but there was no way he was breaking away first. She was soft and warm, melting against him like they'd been born to fit together this way.

For a tiny moment, his scientist brain took over, agreeing that this was a most interesting engineering feat, for two people to match given all the possibilities within the human gene pool.

Then he told his brain to shut up, and he kissed her harder.

Chapter Twenty-Nine

Paige decided air was *way* overrated. She was shaking, she knew that much, but Ben held her so tight that she felt safe. For once in her life, she was going to go with her heart. They wouldn't have much time together before they left for college, but who cared about that when one of his hands was stroking her back and the other was tangled in her hair and the feel of his mouth on hers was making goose bumps rise all over her body.

Nobody had ever made her ache like this—her whole body felt like a live wire, processing every touch. She shifted so she could straddle him. The swing jiggled as she moved, but he kept her steady by keeping his hands on her hips, then groaned against her lips when she settled on top of him. She pulled away and smiled, feeling powerful, knowing she could make him crazy.

"I can't believe this is real," he whispered. "Guys like me aren't supposed to be this happy. Not in high school. We're late bloomers. If we break through at all."

Her pulse fluttered in her neck when he reached up to trace his fingers from her jaw to her collarbone. "And girls like me are supposed to scare guys away," she said. "But here we are."

"Here we are."

They stared at each other for another few seconds, then their mouths crashed together, hungry, searching. His hands slid down her arms, to her legs, then slowly back up again. He couldn't touch her enough, and she whimpered against his lips, begging for something she couldn't define but wanted *right now*. She'd never forget how he smelled — dear God, chocolate and cinnamon — or how hard his body was against the softness of hers. She ached and shivered as his fingers traced a circle on the inside of her palm. Everything had come together and was perfect. She never wanted their time together to end, but if it did, she was happy to have him now.

After a few more breathless, too-short minutes, she reached up to twist her fingers into his hair. He pulled away, blinking and slightly cross-eyed. "No fair. You knew all along that would drive me insane, didn't you?"

She didn't stop massaging his scalp. "It does, huh? I had *no* idea."

He closed his eyes and breathed. By the way his arms were shaking, she could tell she was about to max out his control, so she slid out of his lap and kissed his cheek. "We should stop. In case my parents decide to get nosy."

"Yeah. Okay."

His voice was hoarse, and she barely held in a giggle. "I

probably should fix your hair before my parents see you."

He growled. "You're torturing me now."

"Maybe a little."

Eyes gleaming, he reached for her again, but Mom turned on the kitchen lights, the porch lights, and the pool lights. They squinted at each other in the sudden brightness, and Paige sighed, wondering how much Mom had seen. "Guess it's time to go. School night and all."

Ben kissed the side of her head. "That's okay. I have to be home by ten anyway."

She leaned in closer. "See you tomorrow?"

"Yeah, at school, but I have to work nearly every evening this week. I'm on until seven tomorrow."

She made a noise of protest and he buried his face in her hair. "What are you doing Tuesday? I'm off at six instead of seven."

"Piano recital."

"What time is the recital? I'd like to come," Ben said.

Oh God. Not as if she wasn't wrecked enough about the recital, but now *he'd* be there? "Seven thirty, but I won't play until after eight."

"I'll be there."

"You don't have to come," she said, getting up from the swing.

"I want to."

She shook her head. "I'm going to be nervous."

"Is this about the allegro section?"

Her smile drooped. "I'm still messing it up. No matter how much I practice."

"Slow it down a little," he said. "That might help."

"I forgot you took lessons." She took his hands. "Such

long fingers. Perfect piano hands. Why'd you quit playing?"

"Money. It's okay, though. I'm more suited to building things."

She hated how hard things had been for him, and she stood on tiptoe to give him a hug. "I'm sure we can find another good use for your hands."

He let out a shocked laugh. "Anytime, anywhere, Princess."

Chapter Thirty

Ben

"Princess? Huh." Paige scrunched up her face like she was thinking it over. "I like that one. My dad calls me Sweet Pea, like I'm three." Her face fell. "We won't be home much longer, will we?"

"No," he said, "but we're going to be fine. Neither of us is a quitter. Which leads me to…have you talked to your parents about med school yet?"

She stared at their entwined hands. "No. I did talk to Daddy about staying in Texas, though. He asked me why I was so down yesterday and I kind of blurted it out."

So Dr. Westfield hadn't dug for answers based on Ben's outburst yesterday. Good. "Was he okay with it?"

"Mostly. But not enough that I felt like dropping a second bomb on him." She told him about her time at the center that morning. "I'm not sure I'm cut out to be a doctor, because there's something else, something better, I think I can do for these people. I just don't know how to make him—*them*—understand."

"The right time will come. Just promise me you'll follow your heart. If that's to go to med school, then do it. If not, you owe it to yourself to do what you feel is right."

She hugged him tighter. "I already have."

The back door creaked open. "Paige?" her mother said. "Time to come in."

Busted. He let her go. "See you tomorrow."

She nodded and went into the house, and he started for the gate, but Mrs. Westfield called him back. "A word, please?"

Oh, this couldn't be good. "Sure."

She shut the back door firmly behind her, looking through the window, probably to be sure Paige was gone. Definitely not good. "My daughter is very special, as I'm sure you know."

"She is. She really is," he said.

"And she has a brilliant future ahead of her. So, I'm sure you'll understand when I say that she doesn't need the distraction of a boyfriend right now."

He barely kept his expression neutral. "What makes you think I'm her boyfriend?"

"I may be forty-five, but I'm not blind, Ben. You two were curled up on that swing, and she's floating around our house like some drunk fairy." Mrs. Westfield stood up taller, which was more funny than intimidating. She was shorter than Paige—he could probably pick her up and put her on the roof without too much trouble. "I don't want my daughter to be hurt and lose focus on what's important. Her grades dipped a little after she broke up with Caleb, and I'd rather that not happen again. Perhaps it's a good idea if you two slow things down a bit."

She glanced at his hands and her lips pursed. Was she imaging them covered with grease? Or did she disapprove of the calluses and ragged fingernails that came with his job?

"It really is for the best," she insisted.

Sure it was. "Is this because I'm from the south side?" he asked through clenched teeth. Damn it, he was sick and tired of being judged, of never truly being seen for who he was or who he could be. And it wasn't just him. Mrs. Westfield treated Paige the same way.

She stiffened. "You should leave. And Ben, don't come back to my house."

Damn it, he shouldn't engage her. While it didn't seem to have any negative consequences—yet—he'd already picked a fight with her dad. Did he really need to piss off both of Paige's parents? But his mouth was like a car with worn-out brakes—it couldn't seem to stop no matter what his brain told it. "Why? Because I'm questioning your decision?"

"This isn't about you. It's about my daughter." She held up a hand when he opened his mouth. "Paige has a D in calculus. I checked her grades online while you were outside. She's never had anything lower than an eighty-seven on any assignment. Obviously she needs to focus on school, so she's going to be grounded until her grade improves, which means you can't see each other. Please, show yourself out."

She turned and went inside, slamming the door behind her before he could say, *But I'm helping Paige with calculus!*

What the hell had he been thinking, talking to Mrs. Westfield like that? That was the problem, really—he *wasn't* thinking. But she'd taken that controlling, superior tone, and all he could think about was how this woman reduced Paige to tears, and he couldn't let that slide.

Mrs. Westfield turned off all the lights, and he stood out there in the dark, wondering what would happen to Paige now. How could he help bring her grade up if he was forbidden to see her? Knowing her mother, she'd probably be monitored every second outside of school, with tutors on hand to fix her "math problem." Which was something he could do—for free. He'd been so close to figuring out what her hang-up was with calc, and now they wouldn't let him help her.

A light came on upstairs, and for a moment he saw Paige's shadow framed against the blinds. She'd been so happy this evening. He couldn't let her mom ruin that.

But who could help?

Chapter Thirty-One

Paige hummed to herself while she took the pins out of her hair. Zoey had fixed it for her—and she'd made everything else happen, too. How could she have ever been mad at her?

She picked up her phone to text her: *Thank you. It was a great night.*

Z: *Sweet! How'd you talk him into coming over?*

P: *What? You told him to come over.*

Z: *No—I told you to text him.*

P: *You said you would.*

Z: *No, that's not what I…Wait—I didn't ask, and neither did you…*

Paige held a breath. Neither one of them had asked him to come, which meant: *He came on his own! OMG!*

Z: *I told you. I TOLD YOU. He likes you, silly. Yay! Tell me all about it tmo.*

Paige clutched her phone to her chest. This whole day was a big fat mess, and it still turned out so perfectly. Smiling, she opened the box Ben had given her. Inside was a nest of different cookies: chocolate chip, snickerdoodles, and peanut butter. She'd wanted to eat one when he handed the box over but had forgotten all about it as soon as he kissed her. The note was still on top.

You're the only girl in the room.
—Ben

Warmth stole through her, and a big, goofy smile spread across her face. Everything he'd done—the cookies, coming over here, the way he looked at her—was so amazing. No one had ever treated her like that, like it was *her* turn to be taken care of. Treasured. For once, someone else had done all the work, and she'd been able to enjoy everything without worrying about a single detail.

And he'd done all this without any help—or so she thought until she saw another note tucked under all the cookies. She pulled out a chocolate chip to move it out of the way, of course, and just about melted into a puddle after the first bite. "God. His mother needs her own bakery. So help me, baby Jesus."

She ate two more, you know, to make the piece of paper more accessible, then slid it free from the bottom of the box, careful not to disturb the rest of the cookies. This note was even sweeter than the first, and she could hardly believe it.

Paige—

My analytical boy may not know how to say it, but he really likes you.
—Jenny Franklin

P.S. (I hope you like the cookies. I hear you don't eat enough dessert.)

Paige hugged the note to her chest. Ben's mom was so sweet. She had a feeling the desert of no dessert was about to hit an oasis if she kept seeing him. They didn't have much time until graduation, but she wanted to take her chances and make the most of it. And now that she was going to school in Texas, who knew? Rice was less than two hours from College Station, where A&M was. She could drive over on the weekends to see him.

Her heart fluttered at the idea of spending an entire weekend with him, in a place where they had the freedom to do whatever they wanted. She bet they could fill those hours just fine.

Plus, Zoey had been right—she'd been so focused on making over Ben, she hadn't seen that making herself over was what she really needed. She needed to let go of all the expectations and start doing things because *she* wanted to.

Sometimes life was weird. And sometimes it was perfect. Every so often, it was both weird and perfect, all on the same day.

Someone knocked on her bedroom door. Paige shoved the notes back into the cookie box and hid them under her bed. She didn't trust her dad not to eat them all, and she didn't trust her mom not to throw them away. All that sugar, butter, and chocolate might send her over the edge and ruin any future possibility of decent food for good.

She checked her face in her mirror to make sure it was chocolate free. "Come in."

Mom stuck her head in. "We should talk."

Her tone was firm, and a cold shiver ran down Paige's back. "About?"

She came into the bedroom and sat in the desk chair. Paige took a seat on her bed, clasping her hands together. Based on Mom's expression, this wasn't going to be fun.

"While you were on the patio with that boy—"

"He's *not* 'that boy.' He's *Ben.* Stop talking about him like he's dirt on your shoe," she snapped. "He's smarter than the two of us…maybe even smarter than Daddy."

"I don't care if he's magna cum laude at Harvard," Mom snapped back. "I just checked your grades online. I hadn't done that for a while, so it seemed like time."

Horrified, she leaned away from her mother. She knew. Oh God, she *knew.* "Why did you do that?"

"Because I like to keep tabs on how you're doing. Parents' prerogative. Based on your reaction, you already know what I found out—a D in calculus."

"I know, but Ben's been helping me, and I'm getting better. I made an eighty-two on the homework on Friday."

"Is he really helping you, or is he distracting you from working harder?"

Both? Wasn't that the answer? Because she didn't even need calculus to place high enough in her class to earn a good scholarship from a state school, and Ben kept asking her why she was killing herself. There wasn't any point anymore. She wasn't going to Stanford now.

"Calculus is hard. And I'm thinking about dropping it."

If she hadn't been so freaked out, Mom's scandalized expression probably would've been funny. "Dropping a class? You can't do that. You need the AP credit for Stanford."

Daddy didn't tell her? How could he leave that unsaid? Determination swelled inside her. If he didn't have the balls to tell her, she did. To hell with all her mother's plans. "I'm not going to Stanford, so it doesn't matter. I'm staying in Texas."

"What? Is this about Ben? Are you trying to stay here because of him?" A vein popped out on Mom's forehead.

"No!" She hopped to her feet and put her hands on her hips. "I'm doing it for me! Don't you see? I never wanted to go to Stanford. Ben didn't convince me to stay—I *want* to. All he did was give me the courage to question the map you drew up for my life. It's *my* life, Mom. Not yours."

"And what if we don't pay for it?" Her mom's tone was triumphant. "If you don't pull your grades up and go to Stanford, there will be no money."

Was she kidding? Daddy would never go for that, and besides, the money meant nothing. "So what? I already have recruiters calling from UT, telling me they'd pay for most of my tuition based on my SAT score."

"Where will you live if you go to Austin without our support?"

This wasn't fun anymore. If Mom was going to fight

dirty, then so was she. "My trust fund from Grandma has a clause that releases the money to my control at eighteen if it's used for education, just in case you forgot. Plus, Daddy would never abandon me. You see? I don't need you. For this decision, I never did."

Those ugly words hung between them, and Mom's face went pale. "Fine, but you won't be eighteen until April. Until then, you have to live under my roof and under my rules. You're grounded for the next two weeks, and I forbid you from seeing Ben until you have an A in calculus."

"Didn't you hear me say I was going to drop the class?"

"I won't give you permission, and the school won't let you unless I sign off on it." Mom stood, too, and gave her a stern look before taking her car keys. Then she picked up Paige's phone and shoved it into her pocket. "So I suggest you start working harder on that homework. I'll let your friends know you're grounded. Be ready to leave for school at seven forty-five tomorrow morning. I'll be driving you this week, and next."

After she left, the air seemed to follow her. Paige clutched her chest, trying to hold back the scream of frustration begging to tear free. Did Daddy have any idea what Mom was doing? What did he think about all this? Deep down, she was sure Mom had already informed him of her decision, and that he'd gone along with it. He always did.

What was she going to do? She was practically under lock and key without her phone or car. God, when had her life turned into a live-action version of *Rapunzel?*

Sick, she changed into her pajamas and cried herself to sleep.

Chapter Thirty-Two

Ben

Ben tried texting Paige twice that night. He didn't mention her mom in case her phone had been taken. Good thing, because someone finally answered, saying that her phone would be unavailable for a few weeks. Not long after, Zoey texted to tell him that Paige had her phone and her car taken away. She wasn't just grounded—she was cut off.

He tossed his phone on his extra pillow and lay back with his arm behind his head. So close…they'd been so close. Everything had been perfect, then the rug was yanked out from under them. The story of his life.

Mom knocked, then opened his door. Her eyes were alight with excitement. "Well?"

"I don't know," he said in a hollow voice.

"She didn't like the cookies?" She came in and shoved his physics homework over so she could sit at the foot of his bed. "What girl doesn't like cookies?"

"It's not that. She was really happy with them. No, it's her mom. She thinks I'm a bad influence or something. She kicked me out, and now Paige is grounded."

"What are you not telling me? Because that sounds irrational."

He sighed. "She found out that Paige isn't doing well in calculus. I've been helping her with her homework, but Mrs. Westfield has all these ideas about what Paige should do after high school, and they put a lot of pressure on her. So now they think her trouble in math is because of me."

"That's just stupid, since I seem to remember you having a perfect score on the math section of the SAT."

"They don't care. I'm not good enough for her."

Mom patted his leg. "Does *she* feel that way?"

Embarrassed, he stared out his bedroom window. "I'm pretty sure she doesn't. She seems to like me a lot."

"Are you willing to fight for her?"

"Ma, this isn't a romance novel. Her parents are watching her every move. There's no way for me to stand outside her window with a boom box—seriously, they don't even make those anymore—begging her to run away with me, without getting arrested."

She rolled her eyes. "I meant something a little less Lloyd Dobler. Sheesh, show a kid *Say Anything* one time, and he never lets you forget it."

"Like what, then?" he asked. "I'm all out of shining armor. I'll see her at school, but at some point she's going to start believing them and decide I'm not worth the friction with her parents."

"Then you need to go old school."

Something about her tone and the crafty smile made him sit up. "How?"

Mom went to the door. "I'm going to have to start baking more, and you're going to need a ride after school. Is there someone who can drive you into Dallas tomorrow?"

"Yeah," he said, starting to smile, too. "She drives a BMW."

The next morning, Ben rode to school early, like usual, but instead of looking for Paige, he went straight to Zoey's locker to talk over the plan. "Is Paige here yet?"

"Practicing in the choir room. She's a mess." She shut her locker door and leaned up against it. Her hair swung over her shoulder, framing the tight-fitting long-sleeve T-shirt she wore.

Ben hardly noticed, and the part of his brain that did notice laughed. Not because he was turned on by Zoey's effortless hotness, but because he was comparing her to Paige, and it was no contest. God, he had it *bad*. "I don't want to bother her, then. I'll see her in first period. Are we on for this afternoon?"

"Yeah. I'm out sixth period, so we can leave early. Will your mom be ready?"

"She was already baking by the time I left."

"Good." Zoey squeezed his arm. "It's going to work. I know him—it'll work."

It had to work. "I believe you." He *had* to believe, or this whole plan went down the can. He wanted to wipe his sweaty palms on his pants, but that might ruin his outfit. "Do

I look okay?"

She made a big show of checking him out. He'd put on the chinos and a button-down, and he had the jacket Paige had picked out folded in his bag. "Relax. You look fine."

He nodded, took a deep breath, and went to first period. It took some begging, but he talked the girl who sat between him and Paige into trading him her seat. Mrs. Cinster raised an eyebrow but didn't ask.

Paige slipped in barely a minute before final bell. He sat up straighter when she passed his desk, and she gave him this disbelieving smile. He smiled back, waiting for Mrs. Cinster to dim the lights. They were watching the movie version of *To Kill a Mockingbird* today. He'd already seen it, thanks to Mom's black-and-white-movie fetish, so he wrote a note for Paige instead.

After folding it into a tiny heart shape he'd learned from an online origami video to impress Paige, he leaned forward in his desk, like he was stretching, and brushed her arm. When she turned, he dropped the heart into her hand, then sat back to wait.

For a moment, she just looked at it. He silently urged her to open it, but when she did, he felt his face go hot. What if she thought it was stupid?

Paige put her hand over her mouth, then scribbled something on the paper. Her refolding job didn't put the note back into the right shape, but it made it back to him all the same. It read:

I'm not giving up. Not ever.
— Ben
P.S. Like the outfit? This is my version of shining

armor

Underneath that, she'd written:

My hero.
P.S. I like the armor

He folded the note back into a heart and slipped it into her backpack while she wasn't looking.

It seemed like forever before the bell rang. He went out to the hall to wait for her, and she looked shy when she found him.

"I didn't mean for this to happen," she said. "My parents—"

"I know. And I have a plan."

Her eyes widened. "You do? For what?"

He glanced around to make sure there weren't any teachers in the hall, then kissed her cheek, wishing he could do more. "Trust me."

He left her standing there, smiling at him in confusion. No reason to raise her hopes if this didn't work.

Because it had to work.

Chapter Thirty-Three

Ben all but disappeared for the rest of the day. Zoey was acting funny, too, so by lunch, Paige had to ask, "Okay, what's going on?"

"Nothing," Zoey said, but a quickly hidden smirk told the real truth. "How's your mom?"

She dropped the French fry she'd been holding. "Ugh, don't ask."

"I'm gonna ask anyway. She change her mind about Ben at all?"

Paige's appetite drained away and she shoved her tray to the side. "Not even. She's taking me to some special math tutor after school, then home for a healthy dinner—which probably means tofu and wilted greens."

"Yuck. How about your dad? He say anything?"

She shook her head. "I didn't even see him this morning.

I heard him arguing with Mom about something in the kitchen, but he'd gone out to his car by the time I came down."

"That's too bad."

"You sound way too cheerful about all this. What's the deal? Ben was acting weird this morning, too."

Zoey put a hand over her mouth to stifle a giggle. "He looks nice today."

She was suspicious, but she knew she'd get nowhere with Zoey. That girl had all kinds of secrets, and Paige hadn't unearthed a single one, despite being her friend since eighth grade. "Yes, he does. I'm just sorry I won't see him again until tomorrow. Our classes don't match up, and Mom told me if I wasn't outside within five minutes of final bell, she'd extend my grounding to a month."

Her best friend winced. "I knew the woman was hardcore, but come on. That's fascist."

"Oh, I'm being taught a lesson. Apparently being in the top ten in my class and a reasonably good daughter isn't enough. One whiff of teenage rebellion, and she turns into a prison warden. It's like if I'm not perfect enough, it reflects on her somehow."

"Hey, try not to worry about it before the recital, okay? How's the piece coming along?"

"The allegro is still tripping me up. I tried slowing it down, like Ben suggested, but my fingers just can't get it."

"You still have a little time—the recital isn't until tomorrow. I know you—it'll come together at the last minute and you'll do great." The bell rang. "I have to run. I'm off sixth period, so I'll see you tomorrow?"

Paige waved at her, and Alana came to sit next to her as soon as Zoey left, announced in advance by a bright yellow

Polo dress. "So, have you thought any about the fall social? We really need to start the planning, and I need someone to help me with the theme. I was thinking that…"

Paige tuned her out, nodding at appropriate times but not mustering the energy to care. For once, it was time to let someone else shoulder the load.

"Paige? I asked if you thought a luau theme would be fun. We could have those fake coconut cups and leis—"

"It sounds fine," she said without enthusiasm. "I'm finished with lunch and I, um, need to hit the library."

"But you didn't eat anything!" Alana protested, sounding angry. Probably not about the lack of lunch, but because for once, Perfect Paige hadn't solved someone else's problem.

The rest of the afternoon trudged by, and she went straight to Mom's Escalade as ordered. Mom gave her an edged, cheery smile. "How was your day?"

She turned to look out the window. "It sucked, but you already know that."

"I'm just trying to help. You don't see it now, but you will."

Paige didn't answer, not caring what she thought.

After a meeting with the new tutor—useless—they went home, and she headed straight for the piano. If she practiced all afternoon, Mom couldn't hound her. Besides, she had something more interesting to think about…

What were Ben and Zoey up to?

Chapter Thirty-Four

BEN

After school, and a terrifying drive along the Dallas North Tollway, Zoey parked in the lot outside the medical center. "Office five hundred. Good luck."

Ben stared up at the ten-story glass-and-steel building. The afternoon sun created a blinding glare against the windows on the west side. "Office five hundred. Got it."

"You'll do fine. Be your usual geeky, charming self and make sure you talk up the receptionist." Zoey helped balance the two bakery boxes in his arms. "She's worth the trouble, you know."

"She is." He took a deep breath. "I'll text you when I'm done."

"I'll be here." She gave him a bracing smile. "Now go. The office is only open until four thirty, then he leaves to do rounds at the hospital."

Ben's nod was jerky, kind of like his pulse. What was he *doing*? It had sounded so hilarious and simple when Mom explained it, and Zoey had loved the plan, but now that he was here…holy shit, was he really going to do this?

"Go on!" Zoey called from her car.

Right. Squaring his shoulders, he marched up to the front door of the office building. It whooshed open in a gust of air-conditioned air, and he went inside like he belonged here. A bored-looking security guard watched him pass, then went back to reading a newspaper once Ben pressed the up button for the elevator.

The ride up was much shorter than he wanted it to be, and there he was, just outside a door with a sign that read, Dr. P. Westfield, Neurology.

Ben braced the bakery boxes against the wall with one hand and tugged the door open. The waiting area looked like something out of a fancy hotel, with hardwood floors and leather chairs. Dr. Westfield wasn't doing too badly for himself, was he? He approached the receptionist's window, forcing a smile. Charm, Zoey had said. Would "I'm not a serial killer" be enough?

The woman had gray hair and a kind face. She eyed the boxes. "You look kind of young to be a pharma rep. Are you a courier? Or a patient?"

"Um, neither, ma'am. Is Dr. Westfield in? I, uh, need to talk to him. It's kind of important." He set the bigger bakery box down and handed her the smaller one. "Oh, and these are for you."

Eyebrow raised, she opened the box. "Oh, my. These look heavenly. What did you say your name was?"

"Ben Franklin."

She gave him a lopsided smile. "Are you pulling my leg, young man?"

"Wouldn't dare."

Now she laughed. "Aren't you a little charmer? Okay, I'll let Dr. Westfield know you're here. If he has time to see you, I'll send you back. Otherwise, you'll need to make an appointment."

Ben nodded and took a seat in one of the cushy leather chairs. It was working...and he didn't know whether to be excited or terrified. A carriage clock ticked in the corner, and the walls seemed to close in the longer he waited.

"Ben Franklin?" the receptionist said. She was standing in the doorway to the back office and looked even more interested in him now. What had Dr. Westfield told her? "He'll see you in his office. Second door on the right."

"Thanks," he said, hurrying to stand. His legs felt unsteady and the cookies shifted in the bakery box as his hands trembled.

Dr. Westfield's office was every bit as nice as the waiting room, with the same leather chairs. His desk was enormous...and messy? Huh. Did the Westfields even know how to do messy? He must—because the desk was a disaster of papers, empty coffee mugs, and pens.

Dr. Westfield put down a file folder and took off a pair of reading glasses. "The older I get, the harder it is to see anything."

Ben stood fidgeting in the doorway, not sure if he could go in. "I already wear glasses, so...yeah."

"Ah, yes, of course. Come in, come in. And push the door closed, would you? Ruth is an exceptional assistant, but she does like her gossip."

He did as he was asked, then perched on the edge of the chair across from Dr. Westfield. "I imagine you're wondering why I came all the way into Dallas to see you."

"No, son, I'm not." He sounded tired and a little worn. "I'd guess my wife made a real impression. For the record, I did tell her that it was a bit harsh."

"Then you know she told me I can't see Paige anymore."

Dr. Westfield frowned. "She told me it was until Paige's grade came up."

His gut instinct had been right—Mrs. Westfield was playing all of them. "No, sir. She made it very, very clear that I'm not to have contact with your daughter. I'm here to plead my case, man-to-man."

Dr. Westfield's mouth twitched, but he hid the smile quickly. "I like the sound of that. But, first, what's in the box, Mr. Franklin?"

Ben laughed nervously and handed it to him. "A gift for Paige. But you're welcome to anything in there."

"Oh, thank God." Dr. Westfield pulled a peanut butter cookie out of the box, then paused. Ben knew he had to be reading the note, but he didn't say anything. "Your mother is a hell of a baker."

"Yes, sir."

He took a big bite of cookie and sighed. "That's heaven. I didn't have one yesterday—Paige hid the box. After Diana told me about the grades and the grounding, it seemed unfair to ask for one."

Ben sat up straighter. "Yeah. I saw her at school today, and she looked really messed up. That's what I wanted to talk to you about. See, I would never, ever hurt Paige. I haven't been close to her for long, but I've known her in passing for a while, and she's incredible."

"We certainly agree about that," Dr. Westfield said.

"But there's something I think Mrs. Westfield doesn't know. I'm kind of awesome, too. I just need you to let me prove it."

He bent to pull papers from his backpack, ignoring Dr. Westfield's soft chuckle. "Here." He handed over Paige's last calc test. "I asked her for a copy, to see where she went wrong, so I could tutor her better."

"Wait…that's what you've been doing? Tutoring my daughter?"

"Yes, sir. And if you look at this." He handed Dr. Westfield his calc test. "You can see I know what I'm doing. I was so close to helping her to understand it, but now I'm not allowed to tutor her."

Dr. Westfield was staring at the tests. "Your mathematics skills are quite advanced. Some of these solutions didn't come from a high school class, did they?"

Ben flushed. "No. I follow some math blogs. I know, I'm a complete geek. Even my teacher says so. My point is, saying I'm the reason Paige is failing math is illogical. I didn't even know her well until I offered to tutor her."

"So you're here to pitch yourself as a boyfriend?" His lip twitched again. "Or as a math tutor?"

"Both, I guess."

"To me? You're pitching yourself as a boyfriend to me, on my daughter's behalf?"

Ben fought the urge to shrink back in his chair. "Um… yes?"

Dr. Westfield threw his head back and laughed. It wasn't mean laughter, though—he was either amused or pleased or both. "You are one crazy kid, you know that?"

"Is that an okay to date your daughter, sir?"

He sighed heavily. "I want to say yes. I have to be honest—you have some real balls coming up here to bribe me with cookies. My wife is going to be a much tougher sell. I'll make you a deal. Let us get through the recital tomorrow—both Paige and Diana are very wound up about it—then I'll plead your case." He held up the calc tests. "Can I keep these?"

Ben let out the breath he'd been holding. "Sure. I appreciate it, sir. Thanks for letting me talk to you."

"I have to hand it to you—this is certainly the most entertaining meeting I've had all day. And I promise not to steal any more of Paige's cookies. These will make it home safely to her."

It was all he could hope for. "Thank you."

"My pleasure. Let's just get one thing straight...you make my daughter happy, and we'll be fine. You hurt her, and you might need a good neurosurgeon."

He smiled. "Noted."

Ruth the receptionist was hovering around her desk when he came out, so he gave her a thumbs-up, and she clapped her hands. This story would probably entertain everyone from drug reps to nurses to patients' families, but Ben didn't care. He had a new ally.

And this one had an inside track.

Zoey came screeching up in the Beemer as soon as he cleared the front door. "Well?"

Ben climbed into the passenger seat. "He's going to help, I think. He wants to wait until after the recital, though."

"That might be a problem if you show up. He won't have

had time to work on Mrs. W."

"Don't care," he said firmly. "I told Paige I'd come, and I'll be there."

As they pulled into Dallas rush hour traffic, Zoey murmured, "Good."

Chapter Thirty-Five

After ignoring her mom as much as possible that evening, and enduring a horrifying dinner of quinoa and kale salad, Paige escaped to her room. A knot settled in her stomach, one that didn't have anything to do with her dinner. So much had gone wrong in the last few days, and the allegro *still* wasn't coming together. What was she going to do? Go to bed early? That was the only thing she could think of, and she went to the bathroom to change and brush her teeth.

She was already lying down when Daddy called, "I'm home!"

A few minutes later, there was a knock at her door. "Pea? Do you have a minute?"

"No."

"Aw, c'mon." He knocked again. "I have something for you."

She sat up and turned on her reading lamp, blinking in the sudden brightness. "What?"

The door creaked open, and Daddy came in carrying a large white baker's box. Her heart sped up. With a mysterious smile, he left it on her dresser and put his finger to his lips. "I ate one. Couldn't help myself. But he wanted to make sure I gave you these."

As soon as the bedroom door closed, Paige shot out of bed to open the box. Layers of cookies lay nestled in parchment paper. A label was attached to the inside of the lid. In Ben's handwriting, it read: *Told you I wouldn't give up.*

Tears sprang into her eyes. Even though she was grounded, Ben had still found a way to keep her spirits up. How had Daddy gotten these? He hadn't let Ben into the house, had he? She ran to the window and peeked out. No, no cars. The cookies had appeared like magic.

However it happened, it told her one very important thing: She couldn't give up—or give in—either.

When Paige woke up Tuesday morning, the sight of the cookie box made her feel all warm inside, and that gave her the courage to climb out of bed to start the day. Still, she fidgeted the whole way to school. Daddy had left for the hospital early, so she hadn't been able to ask him about the cookies or when he'd seen Ben. Not that it mattered…it made her incredibly happy, despite her mom's best efforts to ruin her life.

"You're acting nervous. Worried about the recital?" Mom asked.

"Yes." She was, and that was a simple enough answer to keep her from spilling the secret about her mystery cookies. "I'm worried about the allegro section."

"You'll do fine. I'm so proud of the way you've applied yourself, honey. See, this is the kind of focus and hard work that'll raise your grade to an A in calculus. All it will take is a little help, and you'll see."

Some of her good mood evaporated. "And sometimes your expectations are too damn high."

Mom's lips tightened until they turned pale. "There's nothing wrong with high expectations. It makes us try harder. Like the diet. Daddy is looking healthier, and your hair is shiny. Making the extra effort is always the right thing."

Paige clamped her jaw shut. Her hair had everything to do with a new shampoo Zoey had talked her into trying, and Daddy's "healthy glow" probably had something to do with sneaking cookies. They were almost to school, though, and starting a fight now would eat up the ten minutes Mom had given her before first period, probably to further limit her time around Ben.

She hopped out of the Escalade the second it stopped rolling, even though they were at the back of the carpool lane. "Bye."

She slammed the door shut before Mom could say anything else and ran for the front door. She'd wanted time to practice this morning. She'd wanted time to see Zoey and Ben. But because she lived in a not-so-benevolent dictatorship, getting what she wanted was proving impossible, even if she now had the backbone to ask for it.

If nothing else, Ben had given her the courage and the nerve to ask.

She trotted into English seconds before the bell for the second day in a row. Ben looked up from his desk and smiled. It was a smile designed to hit her in the heart, and her cheeks grew warm.

"Paige, could you take your seat?" Mrs. Cinster asked. "We need to start the movie if we're going to finish today."

"Oh, sorry." She scrambled into her desk, totally aware of Ben's eyes on her back. Once the room went dark and Gregory Peck showed up on the TV screen, she pulled out a piece of paper.

How did you send the cookies? Magic?

She folded the note and dropped her hand behind her back, shivering when Ben's fingers brushed her wrist. A moment later, he pressed the paper back into her hands.

Definitely magic, but that's all I can tell you for now.

She wrote back, *Meany.*

Never. Now, promise me one thing—rock your recital tonight.

She smiled. *Always.*

She was still smiling after class, even though he was in a hurry and couldn't stay to talk. Something about Ben gave her the courage to be herself.

She stopped walking dead in the middle of the hallway as an awesome idea hit her. To *be herself.* So what if her mom was trying to control every bit of her life? There was one thing she couldn't.

Chapter Thirty-Six

BEN

"Hey, Franklin. It's almost six!" Jose yelled from the oil-change bay. "Get going, Romeo!"

The other guys grinned at him. He'd made the mistake of telling them about his trip to see Dr. Westfield—he owed them that much for skipping out of work at the last minute yesterday. Even Kent had been impressed enough not to give him a hard time.

Ben put away his tools and handed his case sheet over to another team. Kent leaned out the showroom door. "If that mom gives you any trouble, let it roll off, yeah? You have every right to be there. It's a public place."

"Don't worry. I know exactly what I'm doing," he said.

"Nice. We want to hear how it goes." Kent clapped a hand on his shoulder. "You're a good kid. Anyone who doesn't think so isn't going to be welcome at this shop."

Ben stared at his feet, embarrassed. "Thanks."

They shooed him away, and he rode home as fast as he could. Zoey was picking him up at seven, and he needed to be showered and changed. Mom was already back at work, but she'd left him a note wishing him luck. Everyone was pulling for him and Paige. It was hard to take in—he'd been the underdog every second of his life. It was nice to know, for once, people wanted him to win.

He made it home and cleaned up as fast as he could, hoping the recital went well for Paige. Speaking of which... didn't you give a gift to someone who rocked their piano recital? Flowers, right? He didn't have any money for roses, but...

He glanced at the pot in the sunny corner of the kitchen— Mom's lavender plant. Sure, they looked a little like purple-flowered weeds, but maybe Paige would believe it was the thought that counted. He grabbed the kitchen shears, along with a few pieces of tissue paper, and cut a bunch.

Wrapped in the paper, it *almost* looked like a bouquet, but the lavender still looked more like weeds pretending to be roses. He sighed. One day he'd have enough money to buy her real flowers.

When Zoey honked, he ran down to her car. There was a dozen bright red roses lying on the passenger seat when he opened her car door. Damn it. "Aw, you shouldn't have."

"They're not for you, doofus. You give flowers to performers at recitals. They're for you to give to Paige."

He held up the lavender. "I brought my own. Now, this is assuming her mom doesn't set a blockade to keep me out of the auditorium."

Zoey blinked at the lavender, and...wait. She looked

like she was about to cry. Shit—was his bouquet *that* embarrassing? Maybe he should toss the weeds and—

Zoey grabbed the roses and shoved them into the backseat. "Your flowers are way better. And let me deal with her mom," she said. "I'm good at distractions."

"Really? Huh. You're as full of surprises as Paige is."

She grinned. "You have no idea. Now buckle up."

Zoey sped through the streets of Alderwood. The recital was being held at an enormous church in the center of town. "Someplace with a nice, pretentious grand piano," she explained. "Makes the parents feel good about shelling out all that money for lessons."

By the time they arrived, the recital was about to start, so they crept inside and found seats in the back. The sanctuary, or whatever it was called, was huge. Bright lights focused on the piano as a tiny girl with pink ribbons in her hair climbed up on the piano bench and played "Twinkle Twinkle, Little Star" to polite applause.

Ben scanned his program. There were fourteen players before Paige—she was last. The main event, apparently. No wonder she'd been so worried about fixing the allegro section. All eyes would be on her tonight.

"How many renditions of 'Für Elise' are we going to have to listen to?" Zoey whispered after six players had performed.

"Only one of them played Beethoven."

She gave him a desperate look. "How can you *tell*?"

"Program." He held it up, grinning. "And try not to look like you'd rather remove your eyes with a spoon than listen to them play."

"How about a fork?" she muttered.

Finally, once a fourteen-year-old girl nailed a Chopin sonata, it was Paige's turn. The hall quieted as she came onstage wearing a simple long black dress. She didn't seem nervous at all as she adjusted the bench and pulled her skirt free so she could reach the pedals. Her hands hovered over the keys as she scanned the crowd. He sat up straight, hoping she could see him, and she did. Her smile lit up the room, and all the moms in the audience sighed, "Awww," in unison.

Zoey snorted. "They think she's smiling at her parents."

"Who cares," Ben whispered. "She's smiling at me."

Paige turned her focus back to the piano, took a deep breath, then began. The strains of the rondo section filled the room, soaring clear up to the rafters, and Ben thought he'd burst with pride. She played with utter confidence and didn't miss a note. When she finished, he wanted to jump up and down and say, "That's my girl," but knew it would be rude to interrupt in between two movements of a sonata.

She took another breath, and Ben saw her hands shake. "Come on, Princess. Kill it."

"This is the part she had trouble with, isn't it?" Zoey whispered.

He couldn't even answer. His stomach was in knots for her. If he could take all her nerves so she could play without fear, he would. It was so hard to sit by, watching, waiting, and hoping.

The allegro started out very well. Her fingers flew over the keys with skill, but he could tell she was tense just by how she sat. Her shoulders were stiff, and her hands didn't move with the same fluid confidence as they had during the rondo. The closer she came to those troublesome bars, the more his stomach ached.

She hit the bad spot, and like usual, she stumbled—then stopped playing altogether. For a moment, she froze, staring at the keyboard, and only Zoey's hand on his arm kept Ben from leaping up to carry her away so she wouldn't have to face the embarrassment of all those people watching her fail.

Someone coughed, and another person shifted in a squeaky chair, but Paige still didn't move. Whispers floated up from the crowd, growing louder as seconds passed. Finally, her piano teacher rose and took a step toward the stage.

That's when something changed inside her—he could see the exact moment it happened. Her eyes narrowed, and her expression grew fierce. This wasn't the same Paige he'd seen at school this morning. This was a whole different person, someone who knew what she wanted and was going to take it, period. She flexed her fingers, and he thought she was about to plow through the bad spot and finish the allegro.

But what she had in mind was ten times more awesome.

Cutting a side glance into the crowd, toward the spot where her parents sat, she gave the keyboard a hard smile, then started playing a completely sick version of "Radioactive." It was like nothing he'd ever heard before. Paige's fingers slammed into the keys as if she was letting all her frustration, all her fear, all her perfectionism go. Crashing and burning right in front of everyone and not giving *one shit*.

Zoey let out a whoop of triumph, then clapped her hands over her mouth, laughing. "Oh. My. God!" she mumbled through her fingers.

Ben couldn't even breathe. She'd blown off his doors, his windows, and the second story, too. And the way she was playing? He doubted Chris Martin could wreck a piano like that, and he had a stadium full of screaming fans egging him on. "Is this really happening?"

"Hell, yes," Zoey said. "That is a rock star, ladies and gents. Don't forget to tip your server."

The piano shook under Paige's hands, and he saw red staining the keys. "She's bleeding."

That didn't stop her, though. She played the song all the way through, finishing up an octave, making the end sound almost like a lullaby. When she was finished and the last note died away, she sat there, staring at the red smears on the keyboard, her chest heaving. Then she shook out her arms, stood, and bowed.

For a second, the audience looked at one another, not sure what had just happened. Ben and Zoey leaped to their feet, clapping and whistling. The rest soon followed, especially the little piano students up front, who screamed and carried on like they'd seen a live unicorn.

Mrs. Westfield was fighting her way across her row as Paige came off the stage and started up the center aisle, not stopping for pats on the back. She seemed to have a single destination in mind. Her mom darted out in front of her, looking bewildered. Paige slowed long enough to nod. Then she took off like a runaway bride, sailing up the aisle with her eyes fixed on Ben. Something about how she looked at him made his heart stutter. How mind-blowing could one girl be?

She made it up to where they were sitting and held out her hands. Her fingers were a complete mess, the cuticles bleeding and torn, but she was smiling. "I think they got the message. Let's go."

"Whatever you say, Princess," Ben said. "We're all yours."

Chapter Thirty-Seven

They ran out of the church like they were being chased, but Paige didn't look back—she wasn't ever looking back again. "God, that felt so good."

Zoey jumped up and down. "You were incredible! How long had you been planning that?"

She laughed. "I didn't. That's the thing. This morning, I had this idea that if I messed up my piece, I was going to stick my tongue out at my mom, then walk off the stage, like a *to hell with this* moment. But when I hit the bad spot, I decided I couldn't let her take away what I love so much, and that I was going to stop playing the things everyone else wants me to play. It was time to play what *I* wanted."

Ben put his arm around her waist and pulled her to his side. Being next to him felt like a place she could call home, and she leaned into him. "I'm so proud of you," he said.

"I had to keep him from rushing the stage," Zoey said, grinning. "He was totally going to Prince Charming you right out of there when you froze up. I could just see him swooping in to carry you away."

"Since when is Prince Charming a verb?" Ben asked.

Zoey flipped him the finger. "Since I made it one, Boy-friend Wonder."

God, she loved these two.

Paige glanced at Ben, feeling her cheeks warm. Did he know what she was thinking? From how he couldn't stop looking at her, he might know she was falling for him. "Thank you for being here. Both of you. Knowing you were close by made it easier."

They hurried to Zoey's BMW. Someone shouted, "Paige!" from the front of the church. It sounded like her mom.

"Can we go?" Paige asked.

Zoey unlocked her car. "Yeah. Where to?"

"Anywhere but here."

"Wait! These first." Ben handed her a dozen roses. "They're from Zoey." He rummaged in the back seat. "And, uh, these are from me."

He sounded so sheepish, like his flowers weren't good enough, but they *were*. They were better than ten dozen roses. Her eyes filled with tears. "I love lavender. This was so sweet of you. Both of you."

"Yeah, very sweet," Zoey said, jumping into the driver's seat. "Now let's go."

Ben folded up the passenger seat to crawl into the back, but when he started to pull it into place, she darted into the backseat with him. She wasn't planning on letting him out of her sight for as long as she could tonight.

They pulled out of the parking lot, tires squealing. "Anybody following us?" Ben asked.

"Not that I can tell," Zoey said, zooming around a turn that sent Paige right into his arms. "And even if they were, I could lose them."

She snuggled against his side. " Have you noticed yet that Zoey isn't exactly what everyone thinks she is?"

He kissed her temple. "Yeah. She's a little crazy."

Sitting this close to him was making it hard for her to maintain a conversation. She'd rather be kissing him. She turned to brush her lips against his. "And a totally insane driver."

His smile was slow and sexy. "I kind of like it when she takes hard turns. You end up in my lap."

"Hey, I may be playing chauffer, but I still have ears. *And* eyes." Zoey wagged a finger, glaring at them in the rearview mirror. "Car rules—I don't care if y'all kiss back there, but if I hear anyone moaning, I'm pulling over and tossing you out."

"We'll try to control ourselves," Ben said solemnly, and Paige burst into hysterical giggles, burying her face against his shoulder. He stroked her hair. "How are your hands?"

"Oh, yeah. I'd kind of forgotten about them." But as soon as she remembered, they started to sting and throb. "Ow?"

"Why don't we go to my house? I can pull into the garage so your parents won't know I'm home if they decide to drive by," Zoey said. "We can fix up your hands, then you two can head out to the pool house, or whatever, and I'll hide upstairs and not answer the door in case your dad shows up with a shotgun."

That only made Paige laugh harder. "He doesn't have a shotgun."

"How can he not have a shotgun? It's Texas," Zoey said. "*Everyone* has a shotgun."

They turned back toward the country club and made it to her house before Paige's parents did. Zoey smuggled them inside, then went in search of a first-aid kit.

"We should wash off the blood," Ben said. He took her into the guest powder room and turned on the sink. "Here, let me."

He took her hands and gently washed them, taking care not to touch the raw spots on her fingertips and the jagged cuticles where her fingernails had torn. She watched him while he worked, loving the look of concentration on his face, like this was the most important thing in the world. He was being so careful, but she didn't hurt at all, not while he took care of her.

He dried her hands with a soft towel and turned to her, like he was going to say something. She didn't give him the chance—there was no way she'd wait another minute. She hopped up onto the bathroom counter and pulled him against her. Wrapping her arms around his neck, she pressed her lips against his. He jumped, like he hadn't expected her to kiss him, but he slid his arms around her waist and stepped in closer.

She opened her mouth and teased his lower lip with her tongue. He gasped and slid his hands down to her hips, pulling her as tightly against him as he could, which wasn't tight enough because of her long skirt. God, he made her want to do crazy things, and she had the fleeting idea of pulling the skirt up to her waist so she could wrap her legs around him, but something clattered out in the hall.

"Oh, darn! I dropped the first-aid kit," Zoey said in a loud voice. "And thank the Lord Almighty, because this definitely qualifies as a violation of the no-moaning-in-my-vicinity rule!"

They broke apart and Ben said, "I disagree — no one was moaning."

Zoey put her hands on her hips. "Yet."

Paige giggled against Ben's collarbone. "She has a point."

"Yes, I do! Oh, what the hell. Here." She shoved the first-aid kit into Ben's hands. "Just make sure you shut the door this time, because you definitely need a moment." She eyed Paige's position on the bathroom counter. "Or several."

The door had barely closed before Zoey burst into laughter, saying, "By the way, there *might* be a condom in that first-aid kit. Just saying!" The laughter faded as she went farther into the house, leaving them alone.

"I think she's happy for us," Paige said, leaning toward Ben again for a slow kiss. He pulled away after just one, though, and she mewed in disappointment.

"I'm happy for us, too. But please let me look at your hands. Much as I want to keep kissing you for the rest of the night, I can't stand seeing you in pain." He knelt in front of her to bandage her fingers. "You did a number on these. I haven't seen fingers this messed up since a jack slipped on Jose in the shop."

"They don't bother me," she said, shivering as his fingers trailed against the inside of her wrist. "I'm tough."

"You are." He wrapped her pinkie with a bandage, then smiled up at her. "You're one of the toughest people I know.

You've gotten really good at doing what you want for a change."

She tugged at his hands to make him stand up. "Except for one last thing."

"What's that?"

"Telling my parents what I'm going to do with my life."

He wrapped an arm around her shoulders and nibbled at her ear. "Do those plans include me?"

Even after everything, he still sounded unsure, like he was worried she'd leave him behind. She brushed her lips against his. "Definitely. And I'm going to tell them tonight."

Chapter Thirty-Eight

BEN

After Ben walked Paige up to her house—staying off the porch so her parents wouldn't see him—Zoey met him at the curb in her Beemer.

"Everything considered," she said, "this worked out better than I expected."

He climbed into the passenger seat. "Yeah, it did."

They pulled away from Paige's place. Lights were on all over the house. He wondered what was happening, but he wasn't worried. Perfect, uptight, scared of her own shadow Paige was gone. This new girl, the one he might be falling in love with, was crazy strong...and just plain crazy, too.

"I think she's going to be fine," he said. "I did want to tell you one thing."

Zoey took a turn way too fast, causing the back end of the BMW to skid around the corner, and she didn't look bothered about it at all. "Yeah?"

"It's kind of embarrassing."

"Ooh, the best kind. Do tell."

Ben laughed a little. "Okay, so when I asked Paige to help me get to know you, she said, 'Oh, not you, too.' Because she knew I was only thinking about how you looked."

"Yeah, that would've annoyed me, too." Zoey jerked to a stop at a red light. "So?"

He exhaled softly, letting the tension of the last forty-eight hours roll off. "You aren't who I thought you were. You're so much cooler. I'm glad I've gotten to know you, because we have something in common now."

She nodded. "Paige."

"Paige," he agreed.

"I'm glad I got to know you, too." She turned to smile at him. "You're not so bad, Ben Franklin."

"Thanks. I wish I could've fixed your tires sooner last week."

She laughed. "And I wish I hadn't been such a brat about that. We cool?"

"Yeah." He looked out his window, nodding as they turned down his street. Zoey Miller had been to his house twice in one day, and it didn't bother him at all. His zip code didn't matter to her, or Paige, and it was time he stopped trying to be invisible. He had nothing to be afraid of—or ashamed of—anymore. "Yeah. We're cool. Oh, and that party next weekend? Do I wear a costume or what?"

Chapter Thirty-Nine

PAIGE

"Where have you been?" Mom shouted as soon as Paige walked into their kitchen. She and Daddy were sitting at the table, full cups of coffee in front of them, with both phones out. Based on the notepad with scratched-out phone numbers, they'd been calling around looking for her.

"Out," she said, heading for the fridge. She was *starving*. She hadn't eaten most of the day, and her appetite had come back full force. Must be all the kissing. She bit back a smile. "Why don't we ever have anything good in here?"

"Oh, I'm sorry. Is filling the fridge with healthy food a crime?" Mom snapped.

"Maybe a little," Daddy mumbled. He took a step back and held his hands up when Mom's eyes flew open wide, surprised he'd disagree.

She stomped over and pushed the refrigerator door closed. "Where were you? Were you with that Ben?"

"Ooookay, let's get something straight." Paige crossed her arms and put her most *go to hell* expression on her face. "He's not 'that Ben.' He's Ben, my boyfriend. Think whatever you want, but based on what I know about him, I could do a whole lot worse for myself."

The vein on Mom's forehead stood out again. She really needed to chill, because all the tofu in the world wouldn't save her from a stroke if she didn't.

"Young lady, you do not dictate the rules around here, and I won't tolerate…insubordination!"

"Diana! Jesus, calm down. This isn't a federal crime we're talking about. It's not even insubordination. She's just asserting some independence for the first time, and you shouldn't take that personally. Especially since she's put it off until she was seventeen," Daddy said, rising to his feet. He had a stern look on his face, and times like these reminded Paige just how *large* her father was. "Besides, Sweet Pea is right. Ben is a great kid. Trust me, I know."

Paige looked up at him, curious. "How? You haven't talked to him much."

"Ah, so he didn't tell you." Daddy tapped a finger against his chin. "I was kind of hoping he would, but let's just say any kid who will talk your best friend into driving him to my office in Dallas, just to meet with me unannounced, gets my attention. Especially when he brings cookies."

She covered her mouth with her hand. *Magic*, Ben had said. He was right. "I can't believe he did that."

Actually, yes, she could. He wasn't *that* Ben—he was *her* Ben. A smile spread across her face, and she couldn't hold it back. He had her heart, and it made everything possible.

"He really seems to like you a lot. And he seems to have a good head on his shoulders." Daddy winked. "A head I threatened to remove if he hurt you at all. He agreed that was fair, so we're square."

Mom was staring at them. "Phil, what the hell is going on here?"

"I'll explain everything later. What matters is that Paige and I are in agreement. Oh, and I'm lifting her grounding effective immediately. I have it on good authority that she already has an excellent math tutor lined up, and grounding her for a D in calculus would be counterproductive."

"We're her parents, not her buddies. You can't just undo her punishment because a kid asks you to," Mom said. "She needs structure, not enabling. I've devoted most of my time to helping her reach her full potential, and she's going to throw it away on some…boy?"

"Oh, so my finding a great guy and being happy isn't important?" Paige said, trying to keep her voice calm and level. They needed to know she was serious, and take her seriously. "I'm a perfectionist—just like you—but that's not a good thing, Mom."

"Really? Because it seemed to do well for us so far!"

For a moment, she felt really bad for Mom. She just couldn't let things go. "You can't control the universe—it's a good way to die of a stroke. Just ask Daddy. He'd know."

Daddy shrugged and Mom's face turned red. Tears glimmered in her eyes, and Paige was struck by how the tables seemed to be turning in her direction. Like she was the adult, and Mom was the child needing comforting.

"So nothing I'll say will make any difference?" Mom

asked. "Does my opinion not count anymore?"

"Your opinion always matters to me," Paige said gently. "But I'm my own person. It took a hard lesson to learn that it's okay to say no, to speak up for what I want, to find my own way, and to meet my own expectations—not everyone else's. The guy who taught me to trust other people and rely on their help instead of doing it all myself is the same guy who's going to help me pass calc."

"Diana, she's right, honey." Daddy reached over to squeeze Mom's hand. "It's almost time to let her go, and we've been really lucky to have such a smart kiddo. And, hey, she wants to stay in Texas for school—the more I think about it, that's a bonus. We'll see her more often."

Grateful and relieved, Paige flung her arms around him and gave him a big hug. "Thank you, Daddy, for understanding. Thank you."

He kissed the top of her head, then held her at arm's length. "I've been thinking about something else, though. Something Ben said on Saturday about how I…" He glanced at Mom. "How *we* don't ever ask what you want. That had me stumped, because we talk things over all the time. Then today I remembered our discussion about your psychology class, and I think you were trying to tell me something."

Paige backed away, bumping into the kitchen table, then sat. It was time, wasn't it? If he was asking, maybe he really wanted to know.

"Maybe I was trying to tell you something," she said. "Or both of us, because I didn't quite know it myself yet. All my life, I've wanted to make you proud, because you make me proud. I love what you do for Alzheimer's patients, and how much you care about them. And I want to help them, too, but maybe in a different way. That's why…"

She stopped, scared to go on.

"Why what, Pea?" he asked, never taking his eyes off hers. "It's okay. Whatever it is."

Be strong, Paige. Remember, you were going to do what you wanted for a change. "Okay. Here it is…Daddy, I don't think I want to be a doctor. I'm so sorry—I know how disappointed you are—but I can't see myself being happy as a neurologist. I don't see myself being happy anywhere in medicine. So…I'm not going to medical school."

He nodded slowly, but Mom said, "Wait, I don't understand. This is all we've talked about the last four years. She'll take over the practice after earning her MD. That's the plan."

"I thought I wanted to be a doctor, Mom. I really did. But the longer I think about it…Daddy said a good doctor was more like a scientist, and I'd rather help people. Not with medicine, but…" She remembered what Dr. Geldman had said, about the way she related to patients at the Elder-Care center. "I want to build relationships. I want to solve problems by talking to people and listening to them. I'm good at it. Every time I go to the center, I feel like I'm in the right place. It won't be like that if I'm their doctor. Please, please don't be mad."

Daddy turned sad eyes on her. "Mad? I don't know why you think I'd be disappointed or mad. If I'm hearing what you're saying, and I think I am, you're saying you want to work on the other side of the same problem I'm trying to solve. You're taking psychology and you seem to enjoy it, right?"

She nodded.

"Okay, do you know that every patient I work with needs

counseling? And most of their families do, too? Alzheimer's, senility, brain injuries—those conditions are really hard to cope with. They need someone to help them grasp it," he said. "They need a compassionate, caring psychologist who understands geriatrics and memory care."

A small bloom of hope grew in her chest. "Really?"

"Yes. You could specialize in geriatrics and music therapy, if you wanted to. All that can be done—it'll take graduate school, and a PhD would be best." He laughed. "So, you see, I'll still have my way. You'll still be a doctor. You'll just be a much happier one."

"That sounds perfect." Tears filled her eyes. "Are you sure you don't mind?"

"Mind? No, of course not. I want you to follow that enormous heart of yours. You make me so very proud," he said, sounding choked up, too. "But please tell me you applied to UT and Texas A&M, or at least Rice. Because those would be the three schools I'd pick for what you want to do."

At the words "Texas A&M," her heart took a hard bounce and her hope grew. "No, just Rice so far. But I still have enough time to apply to the other two, as long as I hurry."

"Then I guess you'd better get busy." He took Mom's hand. "Look how her eyes are shining. This is what she's meant to do. I'll find another doctor to take over my practice. We need to let her go."

Mom looked like she might cry at any second, but she didn't say anything. She stared into space, like her entire world had been rocked in the last five minutes.

And in a way, Paige supposed it had.

The silence seemed to last forever, though, and her

nerves frayed at the edges. As much as she wanted to go her own way, she couldn't walk away from this without knowing it was okay. "Mom?"

Mom blinked, and a tear escaped, turning black as it ran through her mascara and down her cheek. "But...this isn't what we talked about. Why is everything changing now?"

"Because I need it to." Paige smiled a little, hoping to soften the blow. "It's time I started making my own decisions and learning from my own mistakes. I can't do that if I let you two oversee every aspect of my future. I need to do this."

"Oh."

Another silence stretched out, and Paige held her breath. Was Mom coming around, or was she too upset to think because The Plan had shattered?

Finally Mom asked, "Are you sure, Paige? Are you sure this is what you want?"

She nodded. "Very."

"I haven't been listening, have I?" Now she started to cry. "I swore when you were a baby that I was going to be this perfect mother, but I'm not, no matter how hard I try. You've been so...on edge, and I thought it just regular teenager stuff. But you were hurting, and it was because we put so much pressure on you. I should've seen that. A better mother would have."

She laid a hand on Mom's arm. "Sometimes you're too hard on yourself."

She let out a choked laugh. "It's only because I care so much. About you and your father. I love you both, and I'd do anything to make sure you succeed."

"That's the thing," Paige said. "I have succeeded. Fourth

in my class, accepted to top-tier schools, planning a career in an area I love." Now she smiled. "Dating a wonderful guy. If that's not success, Mom, I don't know how to define it."

She nodded absently and reached for a tissue on the kitchen counter to dab at her eyes. Paige almost chuckled when she frowned at the mascara on the tissue. They still had a long way to go before Mom let it all go, but maybe this was a start.

She took a deep breath. "If becoming a psychologist is what you want, then you need to follow your heart."

Not a glowing endorsement, but Paige would take it. "I'll do you proud. I promise."

"Oh, I know you will. You always do." Mom finished wiping her eyes. "But there's one more thing we need to discuss—the piano piece tonight."

Oh, great. All this soul sharing and Mom was still going to chew her out? "Yeah?"

Mom broke into a huge smile. "I've never heard anything like it. Why don't you play that stuff at home? Beethoven's nice, but that other song was wonderful."

Her mouth dropped open far enough to catch some flies. "Uh…okay, sure. Anytime. I know lots of songs like that one."

"Great." Mom came to put her arms around her. "I'm sorry, honey. You're a good girl, and I want to do everything I can to keep you safe, healthy, and happy." She reached out for Daddy to pull him into a family hug. "But I think I went overboard, and I can start fixing that. I can't swear I won't still buy kale, but I'll make sure we have real cheese instead of that crap vegan stuff."

Paige laughed. "You hate it, too, huh?"

"It's awful! If you can be strong enough to loosen up on your own rules, so can I," Mom said. "I agree with Dad. You're ungrounded, and Ben is welcome in our house. Please tell him that, with my apologies. He's proved he's worth my daughter's time."

"But the math homework comes first, right?" Daddy asked.

"It will," she promised. "I love you both so much."

"We love you, too," he said. "Now, what do you say we find a Sonic that's still open and get some cheap ice cream?"

Mom walked over to the counter and grabbed her purse. "I'll drive."

Chapter Forty

BEN

Three weeks later, Ben waited after school for Paige. He didn't have to work that afternoon, and he wanted to show her something. Plus, they'd had a calculus test yesterday, and papers were being handed back today. He'd made a ninety-eight—and a request from Mr. Granger to show him how he worked out the answer to number six, because he used a technique his teacher didn't know—but he was more interested in hearing how Paige did.

The bell rang and students poured out of the classroom. Through the doorway, he could see her gathering up her books. Now that the weather had cooled down some, she'd stopped wearing the little skirts that drove him so crazy... but he didn't mind the skinny jeans at all. Nope, the skinny jeans were just *fine.*

Huh, she was smiling. That was good, right?

Paige came out of the classroom and walked straight into his arms. "You'll never believe it."

"You made an A?"

She grinned up at him. "An eighty-nine. Close. So close. I'll get it next time."

"You will. You know what this means, though?" he asked, running some quick numbers in his head.

"No, what?"

"You have an eighty-one in the class now." He took her backpack and slung it over his shoulder. "You, Paige Westfield, have a B in calculus."

She clasped her hands together. "Are you serious?" He nodded and she launched herself at him, sending him back a few steps until he hit the wall. "We did it!"

He liked the sound of the "we" in that sentence. "You deserve most of the credit. You worked really hard for that."

A throat cleared behind them. They separated quickly when they saw Mr. Granger standing there. He shook his head, looking amused. "You know, I'm so proud of her grade, I can't even gripe about the PDA. Just take it outside, huh?"

They nodded and hurried out to the parking lot. Ben pulled her in the opposite direction of her Mustang. "Wait," she said, "I'm parked that way."

Now for his next surprise. "Yeah, but I'm parked this way."

"Parked…" She stopped dead in the parking lot. "Ben Franklin, what's going on?"

He was too excited to keep it in. "I bought a car!"

"Are you serious? How?"

"A recruiter called me from A&M—they offered me a much bigger scholarship than I expected. Between that and grants, I don't need to come up with so much money to pay my way through…which meant I had enough saved to buy Mom some professional baking equipment. And I had enough for *this*."

He grabbed her hand and tugged her over to his used black Mazda 3. "It's six years old and has eighty thousand miles on it. But it runs great, and I know a decent mechanic." He patted the trunk. "Kent and the guys at the shop all chipped in to give me four new tires, too. Now I'll have a car to visit you at Rice."

She walked around the car, checking it out. "It's nice, but you won't need to drive to Rice."

Shock coursed through his limbs. What the hell did that mean? Was she not staying in Texas after all? "W-what?"

Paige smiled at him in a way that told him she was far from leaving him. "You won't have to drive to Houston every weekend. See, I've been accepted into A&M."

He could barely breathe. She was going with him to College Station? "You did? You're coming, too?"

"Yes. There's no way I'm going to school two hours away from you. I love you too much to let you be that far away."

He never knew he could be as happy as he was right now. He wrapped his arms around her. They fit together so perfectly. "Good. Because I love you too much to live without you, either."

Then he kissed her.

Epilogue

ZOEY

Zoey stared at the website. "God, how am I supposed to choose just one flavor? I want all the flavors. Just give me all the cookies and no one gets hurt."

Paige laughed. She looked so cute with her hair pulled back in a curly ponytail and wearing that black sweater. Ben's eyes followed her wherever she went. They were disgustingly adorable and all, but Zoey could barely keep from sighing. She managed to hold it in, though, because this experiment was too important to them. Besides, Mrs. Westfield was sitting next to her.

"I know, right? I need a cookie right now," Mrs. Westfield said. "Ben, you did a great job with your mother's website."

"Thanks." Ben flushed. "She's pretty happy with it."

Zoey found it hilarious that Mrs. Westfield still scared him a little. She was forever looking for ways to make him have to talk to her, just to watch him squirm. "Okay, I'm going to order two dozen oatmeal chocolate chip, and a dozen pecan sandies. My dad loves those."

A few clicks later, Ben checked the iPad he'd bought to help his mom with her business. "Great! The order went through. We can go live tomorrow."

"Excellent," Mrs. Westfield said. "I have yoga and bridge club tomorrow. I'll hand out her business cards. You should see orders start pouring in after that. People are dying for last-minute gift baskets for the holidays."

"Perfect, but we have to stay local for now. Just so they know," Ben said. "I'm doing the deliveries for my mom until her small business loan comes through. With a little luck, we'll be able to open a shop for her next summer when I'm home from school."

"She shouldn't have a bit of trouble drumming up plenty of business around here," Mrs. Westfield said.

Paige looked like she was going to burst with pride at any second, and the only cure would be to get her hands on Ben as soon as possible. Zoey knew she'd better go. "I'm out. I need to pack."

"We'll miss you," Paige said, walking her to the front door. "It kind of sucks that you're always gone for Christmas break."

Zoey faked disappointment—this annual trip was the best part of her year. "I know. Aspen is full of poseurs, but the skiing is decent. I'll see you the Sunday before school starts." Then she winked at Paige. "By the way, I told my mom that you would look after our house while we're gone, bring in the mail and stuff. The key's on your kitchen table. Don't forget where that first-aid kit is. It's still *fully* stocked."

She hurried down the sidewalk to the sound of Paige's shocked laughter. She really was happy for them, but it only underlined how lonely she was. Hell, she knew it was a self-imposed loneliness, and Ben had been trying in vain to set her up with a number of his adorkable friends. They didn't understand why she never said yes, and she wasn't about to tell anyone the real reason, because it was a little weird.

Her phone buzzed in her pocket the second she walked through her front door. "You packed yet?" Mom called from upstairs. "We're leaving at five a.m., and we need to be ready to go."

"I'm going up now," she shouted back, fishing her phone out.

Parker: *We're here! Mountain's great! See you tomorrow?*

She smiled. Next to Paige, Parker Madison was her most favorite person in the whole world…except maybe his older brother Luke, but he was a different kind of favorite.

Z: *Yes. I'm packing now. Should I bring that super-ugly sweater with the reindeer on it?*

P: *If you don't, Luke and I will call you a coward. You swore you'd wear it. Srsly, we'll bawk like chickens every time we see you, so bring the sweater, Miller.*

Okay, add one ugly reindeer sweater to the packing list. At the mention of Luke, though, her fingers trembled. Just his name had her hot and bothered—the only guy for the last two years who could even make that claim. She'd had lots of offers, but no one here was anything like him.

Z: *I'll bring the stupid sweater. Tell Luke hi.*

She climbed the stairs and pulled out her suitcase. This was going to be the winter break when she finally landed Luke Madison. You could bank on that promise.

Because she planned to make good.

Acknowledgments

Before I start saying my thank-yous, can I just say that this book was a joy to write? Every manuscript has its struggles, but this story hit me straight in the heart the second Heather Howland asked me if I wanted to write it. I hope you loved it as much as I do.

Now, I'd like to acknowledge and profusely thank:

First, you, the readers. Without you, this book never would've had an outlet.

To Heather and the Entangled Crush editing team, for the encouragement and great feedback. It's been a wonderful experience working with you on this book.

To Kary Rader and Becca Andre, my awesome beta readers, for your help and insights. My work is always better for it.

To my kiddos, you two rock. Both of you are growing more amazing every single day.

To my parents, who had a "Perfect Paige" on their hands

but saw through it to find the real girl and help lighten her load whenever they could.

Finally, to Ryan—you're my geek in shining armor. Here's to another twenty years.

About the Author

Kendra C. Highley lives in north Texas with her husband and two children. She also serves as staff to four self-important and high-powered cats. This, according to the cats, is her most critical job. She believes in everyday magic, extraordinary love stories, and the restorative powers of dark chocolate.